IF YOU WANT ME TO STAY

ALSO BY MICHAEL PARKER

Hello Down There

The Geographical Cure

Towns Without Rivers

Virginia Lovers

IF YOU WANT ME TO STAY

TO STAY

MICHAEL PARKER

ALGONQUIN BOOKS OF CHAPEL HILL   2005

Published by
Algonquin Books of Chapel Hill
Post Office Box 2225
Chapel Hill, North Carolina 27515-2225

a division of
Workman Publishing
708 Broadway
New York, New York 10003

This is a work of fiction. While, as in all fiction, the literary perceptions and
insights are based on experience, all names, characters, places, and incidents
are either products of the author's imagination or are used fictitiously. No
reference to any real person is intended or should be inferred.

Library of Congress Cataloging-in-Publication Data
Parker, Michael, 1959–
    If you want me to stay / by Michael Parker.— 1st ed.
      p. cm.
    ISBN-13: 978-1-56512-484-4
    ISBN-10: 1-56512-484-7
    1. Boys—Fiction.   2. Brothers—Fiction.   3. Soul music—
Fiction.   4. Runaway wives—Fiction.   5. Motherless
families—Fiction.   6. Mentally ill fathers—Fiction.   7. North
Carolina—Fiction.   I. Title.

PS3566.A683I35 2005
813'.54—dc22   2005041093

10 9 8 7 6 5 4 3 2 1
First Edition

This book is for Emma

ACKNOWLEDGMENTS

Thanks to the University of North Carolina at Greensboro for a research leave during which this novel was written; the National Endowment for the Arts and the North Carolina Arts Council for their support; and the editors of *Shenandoah*, in which a portion of this book first appeared. Much thanks also to Janet Peery, Peter Steinberg, and Darcey Steinke. Huge thanks, finally, to Kathy Pories for her kindness and wisdom and unflagging faith in things that matter most.

IF YOU WANT ME TO STAY

ONE

THAT MORNING MY DADDY went off for the worst time, I was listening to some Rufus Thomas. "Push and Pull," I believe it was, or maybe it was "Walking the Dog"? Both of them feature a saxophone sounds like it's sliding up-side you in bed on a bone cold night, and look—there are just certain songs which, look, if you hear them and your ass does not in anyway respond, I am talking not the slightest slow-twitch muscle memory if you're old and the minimal sway if you're still young enough to shake it, well, look—it's hopeless. Give it up. What is even the point?

I had Rufus turned up loud while I fixed breakfast for my little brothers. Froot Loops and canned peaches which Carter likes them drained and Tank cares nothing for the peaches themselves, he's all over the syrup. Ten in the morning and Carter and Tank were playing up under their bed with soup spoons to catapult plastic army sergeants up into the box springs. I had called them and I had called them.

I stood in the kitchen, moving to Rufus. It occurred to me

to wonder where my daddy was but when he's All Clear he likes to get up early and mess around outside. He's got a vegetable garden going every season he's well enough to get something in the ground good after the last hard frost. Me and Tank and Carter, we used to help him out hoeing and especially watering which we liked because Tank would plant his sergeants in the furrows and we'd flood their asses head over heel down out of there when the levee broke high up in the pretend mountains (there being nothing higher than an anthill within fifty miles of our corner of southeastern North Carolina) flooding also in addition to the sergeants, Tank's namesake tanks, my long-gone older sister's troll dolls, Cracker Jacks we would be eating to keep up our strength while hoeing and watering and whatever else pack-rat Carter would stick out there to get obliterated by the awesome force of nature. But sooner than later it turned itchy and hot out in that garden and my daddy would tell us it's okay boys y'all are now officially off the clock and we'd get on our bikes and take off. Bye now, Daddy, you better put on some sunscreen! He'd holler back at us to be sure and hydrate. We might see him again in an hour or sometimes not until suppertime, it did not matter when he was All Clear.

The Froot Loops were puffing up, pink-milk-soaked for nearly an hour while I did not bother looking out for my daddy and called to my brothers who did not come and did not come. Could have been they hollered something smart-assed back at me. Likely I had turned up Rufus even louder, was walk walk walking that dog or doing that dance they call the Push and Pull. All I know is somehow I felt it, through the sweet saxophone and a rhythm section so slaphappy it slung water out of the muddy Mississippi all over them boys' breakfasts when I went to pour some milk in their glasses: the end of the All Clear in my poor daddy's head.

I went in the bedroom I shared with Tank and Carter and found them up under the bed with soup spoons acting like they had never heard somebody calling their names. First I tried to coax them out but then it got even louder, end of All Clear. Rufus fading like my daddy had ahold of the dial, and I dropped down on the floor and slid in under there to where I could grab Tank by the scrawny shoulder and yanked him out and told him to run outside, wait for us in the yard. Then I did the same for Carter, who put up more of a fight because he's more of a fighter. I had him by the bygod hair by the end of it which, he loves his long yellow hair. Grabbing hold of it is a last resort but it works like last resorts are supposed to until they don't anymore. I can't say whether there was something else I could have pulled to make his hair a next-to-last resort. I would like to think there is always say another something to do to get someone to act right but then growing up with my daddy when he was half the time gone off and my sister who seems like she got to the bottom of her patience for all of us around the time she learned to cuss and my mama who had left by that time too, it's hard to believe people have a little bit of themselves on hold like what my mama called her mad money, stashed away in a secret place for when you dearly need to spend it. When it comes down to it, though, you're better off using yourself as an example than you are other people and it seems like I am the type that will put up with right much so long as I think the person I'm putting up with is mostly worth it. Lots of people including the great soul singers of the sixties and seventies me and my daddy and Carter and Tank so dearly love have made mistakes in their lives or got mixed up in some trouble they never left out of their houses seeking. Myself I like to listen to what all that mistake-making and I-didn't-seek-you trouble has left in the way of I think they call it a legacy. I know that somebody stood fast by the singers of my sweet songs.

I got those boys out in the yard and then into the truck in flat seconds. Usually, too late was what it was when the rumbling started in my daddy's head. Sneak close up on him when he'd gone off and you could almost hear it in there, distant like a TV turned too up in a blue buzzing house you pass by down a dark street. Sometimes I could feel it building from the next room over. I'd need to get us out of the house before he blew. Else, hide.

Now when I think of that last time, it feels separated into little here and there boxes. I have to tell it the way it comes to me and that day, now, feels broken, not one continuous song like what happened afterward but more like someone's tuning a radio and stopping to seek out a chorus or a guitar solo, then getting impatient or bored and moving on to the next station.

Daddy'd parked full out in the sun. It was boiling. Ten in the morning and I had not yet got those boys to eat any breakfast.

I grabbed the wheel of the pickup like I was going to haul us out of there for good. Like my sister, and my mama. Sheriff Deputy Rex when he come for us next to last time said, "You poor boys. Must be awful stuck way the hell out here by yourselves when your pa goes off his rocker." "No," I said (knowing by the way he said "rocker" he wasn't the one going to save us), "it teaches me go on ahead do it now, don't wait until you're in bed, lie awake forever worrying why did you not."

"Why did you not do *what?*"

"Whatever it is needs doing," I said. I could see I had confused the man. He shook his big slow head. Sheriff Deputy Rex you could tell did not suffer sheriff deputy training to be carrying three dirty boys around to county agencies after a neighbor called to report their daddy was out in the yard howling at dead dogs again. It was not manly and we boys hummed (When was the last time y'all came upside some soap? asked Sheriff Deputy Rex.) and besides, unless our daddy actually went ahead and bodily harmed or sexually messed with us which he wasn't about to ever do we always ended up back down in the country with him. Sheriff Deputy Rex said several times he knew my daddy and liked my daddy when he was acting right in the head that is but he had never actually laid eyes on my mama. He said it in a way suggested there wasn't any mama, which got away with me big-time. I said, "You want me to describe her to you?" He said, "Shoot." I said, "She's got gold hair and shiny green eyes but the rest of her's like underwater, you know?" Mr. Sheriff

Deputy Rex studied my brothers in the rearview mirror then looked at me over his boxy shades and said, "Oh, okay, I hear you, bossman."

In the truck I tuned out Tank and Carter's growling stomachs and said to Mama, I don't relish sky. Bottom of the ocean's nothing to me but wet ridges, flooded old stubbly cornfield. Other people's mystery places ain't nothing to me. Places I crave are attic and basement. Dark and secret, filled with things people think they don't need anymore.

Ma, I want a basement, I said.

Don't say ain't, she said. Baby, look: down there so close to the ocean it'd fill with water before you could shovel out the sand.

Maybe where you're at then?

She sends me her address and I climb down off the train and shuffle along crowded sidewalks until I hear her voice floating down from way up in some hotel. Darling, come right up for iced tea and Fig Newtons!

I climb all out of breath up there. I don't want doors closing on me I can't open, so no elevator for me. She's standing outside her room fully dressed under I think you call it a kimono. The lobby smells like elegantly got-up people who live irregardless in tiny rooms and cook soup on red electric coils.

I say to Ma waiting in the hall, How come you up and left us out there alone with him?

Don't cuss, I swear I'll fall apart on you if you cuss me, she says.

It's my sister who's got the foul mouth, I ain't about to cuss her.

Then she says (louder, as if I'm going to have trouble understanding this), I worried it might spread.

It ain't the chicken pox, I tell her.

Isn't, she says. See, Joel Junior, I slept beside your daddy and it got to where I could hear it in there even when he was All Clear. I'd put my ear up to his, hear that conch shell roar.

So you took the TV and left us there with him?

No, hell no, honey, that's not what happened. He took a golf club to that box to rid it of what he said were corrupt law enforcers. See, I got to where I could hear it all the time. I was always expecting it, even when he showed no signs of going off, even when he was the sweetest, funniest man I loved in this wide world.

So you were thinking it was better just to leave us to deal with it?

Y'all go outside and play, she says, which is what she always used to say to any one or all four of us whenever we asked her something she did not much want to answer. She goes inside her room and I follow and she lights a cigarette off a candle. A candle? Who burns one not in a state of emergency? I was thinking she had her new candlelit, high-up-in-some-hotel life and it won't real, while back in the truck Tank and Carter were wanting to know why Daddy woke them up early hollering out in the yard at the neighbor's been-dead dog.

We sat in the truck, doors locked, windows shut. Inside, Daddy had taken his hunting knife to the mattresses again looking that money, that money. He brought the stuffing out of the mattress in handfuls onto the porch where he washed his hands of it, I'm through with you, cotton! Tank, watching mattress guts fluff off Daddy's fingers into the daylilies Mama planted in the dappled dirt where the gutters dump rainwater during a storm said, "Daddy's snowing."

Mama, if it's catching we will get it, I say.

She says, Oh no baby you won't either it's not something would dare inhabit a child.

Once I asked my sister before she left what in the world was wrong with our daddy and she said when she was little our mama left our daddy and took his pickup and found another man to get with. She said this was what was wrong with him, having to see his wife's boyfriend driving his own blue truck with the MY CHILD IS AN HONOR STUDENT AT TRENT HILLS ELEMENTARY SCHOOL sticker around town. He didn't say nothing, according to my sister. He just shrugged whenever anyone asked him about it, said, What can you do, jack? Then my mama came back to him and had more babies but it was too late, the pressure had built up in his head.

"Un-unh," I said. "You're a lie."

"What do you think it is then?"

"I think he was born that way."

"You better hope not," said my sister, and I asked her what she meant but she was through talking to me about Daddy's problems and pretty soon she was through with all of us.

UP IN THE CAB of the pickup some Pop Rocks Carter had stashed in the seat cushion and half a crumbly pack of Nabs were all we had for lunch and supper too. Thank goodness for the empty Coke bottle and the empty quart of oil in the floorboards. Already Tank was twisting and grabbing his mess and after a little bit of this he squealed *I got to go* and I made Carter hold the quart of oil while Tank filled it with his bubbly pee. Carter wasn't happy with this assignment. He said he won't holding no pee bottle. I told him if he didn't he could go back inside, hang with Daddy. Sometimes I talked awful to Carter but not really to Carter, he was just standing in. But he didn't know that. He turned his head and held the god-durn bottle. I told Tank stick his skinny thing up to the mouth but don't go down in it. Don't get stuck now, I told Tank. Carter's head was turned but I heard his smile. Flies buzzed. Plastic thundered as he let rip.

Tank fell asleep with his mouth open. His pee quart frothing on the floorboard. Carter caught me mumbling.

"Who you talking to?"

I screwed up bad. I said: "Mom."

"Mama?"

"Babies say *mama*."

"Where's she at?"

My eyes went lazy-slack. I came close to saying, "Y'all go outside and play."

But I said nothing because soon it would be dark down at the edge of the lawn and the woods would creep up the grass in bushy shadows. When the darkness reached the hood of the truck, no lights on in the house and two little boys both scared of the dark, what was I going to do? I thought about this and how I could not be talking to my mama, day or night dreaming about basement, attic, up-under-the-eaves, sump pump, cave cricket, crawl space. But have you ever tried to stop your mind from going where it believes it ought to be? Like a dog digging a sleeping hole up under a shade bush, my mind kept seeking out that cold secret sand.

CARTER FELL ASLEEP TOO, then Tank drooled his arm awake and the two of them, sweaty and sleep-drunk, started to sing. Tank's squeaky soprano climbed up on some Curtis. He sang about you don't need no baggage, just climb on board that train. He winged up high and sweet just like Curtis, copied right off Daddy's favorite album, *The Very Best of Curtis Mayfield,* the one record he won't mind if we play three times in a row even though once he brought his friend home from a job he had making church steeples and him and his friend were drinking beer and we were blasting Curtis and his friend said, You like that soul music?

My daddy laughed and laughed. He didn't care if he wasn't supposed to be liking Curtis. He didn't care that we were white and that all the singers of songs we favored were black. He used to say black people had got it all over white people and he even preferred their company. But when it came right down to it my daddy didn't hang with anybody except us whether he was gone off or All Clear. He had a few buddies used to come by the house but they never stayed long. You'd see them once or twice and then never again. He had some brothers but they never came by the house either or called him up to wish him happy birthday and we never went and visited them on Sundays or Christmas. I don't believe I could even tell you their names, which I cannot imagine the offspring of, say, Tank, not knowing my name.

Tank got "People Get Ready" taken right out from under him when Carter dropped us right down into "Superfly." We did a few verses of "Superfly," then Carter made that guitar chug with his tongue, announcing Mr. Hot Buttered Soul himself. He said, Shaft he a bad mother hush your mouth I said then here came Tank: I'm talking about Shaft.

All three of us said it together so loud I would not doubt Daddy could hear us: *John* Shaft.

THE WINDSHIELD WAS a movie screen. I described everything to my brothers: mountains and a castle and spotted horses and maidens in a hay field wearing dresses that lace up at the chest like my Chuck Taylors. There goes Grandpa on the *Beverly Hillbillies* chasing after Lady Godiva, there's Mama and Daddy watering a garden and then sitting up on the porch stairs, her one step down, his knees pinching her tight to where she can't go anywhere.

IN THE GLOVE compartment Carter found two of Daddy's wobbly old water-stained cigarettes. Because Carter's an old root hog he knew there were matches on the dash under the drift of receipts, napkins, newspaper circulars listing what's on sale.

He held the matchbook up to the cigarette and looked at me.

"Go ahead light it up, be just like him see do I care."

Carter held the cigarette in his hand, twisting it.

"Dragons if you ask me have smoke coming out of their mouths, not people."

Carter twisted off the filter and the brown leaves pelted the floorboard.

I HAD AN OLDER SISTER, she left, she couldn't take it. She said, If this is love I'm joining the motherfucking carnival.

Tank and Carter missed her but I tried to act like she was ill at everybody all the time which she wasn't. She could make somebody laugh. Once when she was about Carter's age she got mad at Mama and Daddy and ran away and when they caught up to her at the Family Mart playing pinball and asked her where she was headed anyway, she said, On a goddamn diet, and smacked the gum some old boy had bought her.

IN DADDY'S TRUCK: duct tape from when he used to go to work as an assistant. He assisted: carpenters, plumbers, pipe fitters, surveyors, farmers, roofers, ditch diggers, pulp wooders. He could assist near about anyone doing near about anything. I believe he could have done most of it himself, could have hired him some assistants, but there was the pressure in his head.

Plastic curly rings from when you open a thing of milk.

All these receipts. What's he doing, fixing to file his taxes?

A couple of tapes: Creedence which don't work anymore or I'd have it blasting and the Sound of Philadelphia featuring Teddy Pendergrass and Gamble and Huff. Miles Davis's *Sketches of Spain* which he used to put on whenever either Tank or Carter would not go down and he'd put one or both of them in the pickup, ride them around listening to some Trumpet Jazz, which always worked. Mama claimed it was a miracle. According to her I never had problems going to sleep, never fought it. She said I must have been born tired. What it was: I'd close my eyes and a whole other world would start to spin and I'd hang on and dearly hope.

I'M NOT THINKING I'm going to go to college. I might get me a job counting stuff like nail clippers in bins. Dip your hands in a sink of cool metal. You will probably find me living out in the middle of some field or in some trees on the backside of a hill or near a train-track trestle or some broken-windowed warehouses. I will be up in there all alone. People might ask are you lonely? They might stick their head in my window. Might chuck dirt clods at signs out on the road in front of my house. I'll be behind the curtain smiling.

• • •

TANK AND CARTER were hot, hungry, tired, aggravated, smelly. I could not distract them. They wanted out of that pickup.

"We haven't seen him in an hour," said Carter. "He's sleep."

But there was no telling. When it ran its course he drifted off from the awful strain of it. Like running a marathon, I heard him tell Mama once. Slept like he was dead for twelve hours and when he woke up he did not know squat. Blacked out like a drunk man.

Except he was not a drunk. With his work friends he'd drink a beer to be polite but you could tell he didn't like the taste of it, sipping it, holding it finicky up against his chest. He's a good man, my daddy. Did you know that in the fall he'd sign us out of school and load us up in the pickup and drive us to Raleigh for the state fair? And in the winter he'd turn right around drive us back up there for the circus? Sometimes we'd all ride over to Wilmington to attend SuperFlea and my daddy would know nearly all the people running the booths, whatever it was they were selling, old Coke signs or cassette tapes or Depression glass, he'd have them talking about favorite breakfast meat. I knew my mama loved my daddy. She must not of been feeling too good about herself right along the time of that broken up day, her one girl set up any place will tolerate her foul mouth and her three boys locked in a boiling pickup out in the no-tree-plantedest yard in the whole state and her high up in some hotel talking on the phone to some girl from work about I don't know shoes or what kind of food you ought to order on a first date with a stranger.

I knew she knew we were out there. If people loved you and you were in trouble that trouble rumbled in their stomach. They'd be driving along and get a ice-cream headache telling them you were in need. Happened to me whenever Tank or Carter ran off in the woods and Carter came up on a bee's nest which, he was violently allergic, or Tank got chased by some wild I'll-eat-any-damn-thing dog. People if they loved you, they had to leave though. Don't ask me why, it don't make sense to me, it's just something that happens. But see, I must not could love right. I would not leave my little brothers there with him and I was for damn sure not about to let Sheriff Deputy Rex take them.

Tank said, "He's sleep."

Carter pried up the door lock and put his hand down to open the door. Myself I slapped the merciful Jesus out of that boy. About Jesus and all, I don't think so, but what I like is prayer, even if it's just singing or moaning while chewing the edge of your pillowcase when you're fixing to flood the sheets with tears.

Tank went to thrashing so I slapped his mess too. Then it was a tangle and crisp hot slaps on sweaty skin and grunted cussing of boys too young to know how to cuss and Carter pulling up the lock and me locking it back down. Finally he got it up and opened the door and flew out across the sandy yard up the steps into the dark-mouthed house.

"Holy moly," I said.

Tank went to wailing. I hugged him quiet. He was shaking so hard the springs in the seat were singing.

I had to crack the window wider because me and Tank, waiting to see what was going to happen, breathed up all the oxygen. It was straight nervous fumes up in there. Tank's quart had gone to really humming. Neither of us could breathe good.

Then Carter came strolling out on the porch. Screen door slapped his leisurely ass like it'll do a slow old back-leg-dragging dog. He held his hands up All Clear.

"He ain't even in there," he hollered.

Tank made a noise in his throat, a half-strangled hiccup, when we seen the shadow darken the rusty screen. Carter was shrugging and fixing I could tell to strut his cocky stuff, *I told you so, son, us sweating away in that pickup all day and he ain't even in here.*

Daddy had Carter in a headlock before the screen door popped closed. Carter stared sadly at the bunch of bananas Daddy was carrying. With his free hand Daddy put the whole bunch up to Carter's mouth. "Eat, monkey," he told Carter.

Tank was up in my lap, wedged hard against the steering wheel. He had his arms around my neck and I could feel the laughter welling up in his slight little chest. It vibrated and spilled out across the cab.

"Eat monkey, eat monkey." Carter opened up his mouth, took a peel-and-all bite.

"Let me hold one of them bananas, Cart, I'm starving," said Tank. He laughed and laughed.

"Shut up now," I told Tank. "That ain't funny."

Daddy crammed the banana stem in Carter's mouth. Carter's face was wrinkly red. Tank's crazy laugh sucked continuous into sobbing.

"What's he doing what's he doing what's Daddy—"

"Hush," I told Tank. But he wouldn't so I squeezed so hard he choked. I don't know why. I guess because I knew I had to get out of the truck and stop Daddy and let me ask a question: What about those people who leave you with some sweet, ancient, set-in-their-ways, been-years-since-they-even-thought-about-children grandparents and claim they're going to come back for you and you don't hear jack from them for going on, what's it been, eight or nine months? What about somebody who would drop you off one Friday at dusk and act like they'll see you in a matter of days and then don't even write or call or nothing? Who do they think they are? I felt Tank choking under my squeeze, looked over at Carter choking on bananas not ten feet away and I wondered why in the hell she ever named me after my daddy.

Daddy had somehow one-handedly wrenched off his belt. He snapped the fat buckle against the porch boards. I let go of Tank and for a few seconds he was quiet, too stunned to know I'd hurt him. I was big-time wishing his silence would linger.

Daddy had Carter up against the porch column, tightening his arms to his sides with the belt. Daddy was singing a loud tuneless something out of his head. I did not recognize it. I had not a clue about that song out of my daddy's head.

My lap grew warm and wet. Tank said, "He's got some

scissors," and I looked up into Carter's eyes, wild, trying to search out mine. I wanted to roll down the window, say, *I told you to stay in here with us*, but I could not say a word even to Tank who was crying all out of breath, "Joel Junior, Joel Junior."

Carter's yellow hair, wavy down to his shoulders, turned porch boards into carpet. Daddy's singing got louder. I did not understand note one.

Carter's eyes switched off. Any hope I would save him leaked right out of him. I could see it, hope sifting off the porch like cigarette smoke while I sat in warm stinking pee. Tank took to shivering. I palmed his forehead to see did he have a fever. Then he said the word "mama." I said: "Babies say 'mama.'" I said, "Anyway, that's only a word." He wailed, not like a seven-year-old, but in that desperate hilly way toddlers cry when something gets taken away from them. Blood dripped down Carter's neck. Train's brakes sighed and sighed as it slung right into the station. I said, "Let's sing some Curtis, Tank. I ain't going nowhere. I ain't leaving on that train. It's *been* decided, everybody knows it, I was born this way, I'm awful at love."

TWO

GIVE IT UP won't y'all please for the Greatest All-Time Hits of Sweet Soul Legends. Slow jams to melt your bones, throwdowns to make you shake it. You can let your mind wander since there's one song right after another, and besides, what is music for if not to make you remember?

Some things I remember now that I did not yet explain:

Tank had this Tonka toy tanker he used to pine for nights in his crib. Stuffed bears and blankets bored that boy. He clung to the bars of his cage, rattling that crib, walking it toward the middle of the room, wanting his tank. All night long he cried out for it. Used to it would have taken a graduation ceremony or an emergency room accident for me to remember his real given name which is bygod Lawrence.

Carter dearly loved his long yellow hair. So did some girls love that hair.

The last and worst of it is that whole afternoon in the boiling truck I had the key to the pickup in my pocket. Soon as my daddy showed signs of going off I grabbed the keys off the mantel like I always did. Sitting in the truck, singing Curtis and "Theme from *Shaft*," the keys melted into my thigh like keys'll do, a lump no more noticeable than kneecap, elbow. I forgot all about them being up in there. They were just a part of me like the not-good-at-love part. But Carter's eyes were switching around looking at mine and I couldn't help him but nor could I leave him, being so sorry at love. My mama, good at it, called to me to come by her hotel room. I had a choice to make: go to her and get in the process good at love or stay where I was, which, I had those keys in my all-day-long pocket and could of at any time pulled them out and cranked up that vehicle and driven us all three off down Moody Loop. But where to? See, I did not want Tank or Carter along when I next laid eyes on my mama. I had questions I wanted to ask her in strictest privacy. All alone up in some motel room, iced tea and Fig Newtons.

Yoohoo, Joel Junior, up here, my mama called down from her room. So I pulled the key out of my pocket and held squealing Tank down in the seat and got him buckled and fit the key in the ignition, cranked the engine, dropped that baby into gear, and dug deep dual trenches in the yard leaving out of there.

I might have only been fourteen but I knew good and well how to drive. When our daddy (and we love our daddy) was golf-clubbing evil infiltrators out of television sets we would help ourselves to his big thicket of keys and drive up to 692 which we lived just off of, down a dirt road called Moody Loop.

Tank wailed till 692 when Frosty's cinder-block store with the pink polka dots stenciled on the side rose above the corn-fields. Tank at the sight of it said he wanted a fried pie please.

I knew right then I'd have to leave him somewhere. I couldn't keep him. I'd left Carter and now I knew I'd have to leave Tank too behind.

"Also some Funyuns," said Tank. He went on down his list. "Squirrel Nut Zippers, a whole handful. That's dessert if I eat all everything else."

I believe he licked his lips and that I heard the licking over the rumble of the truck and the windows open, blowing all the receipts around the cab. Crazy little off-his-rocker fucker.

"You need your diaper changed," I said.

"I don't wear no damn-it diaper," he said. He couldn't cuss for spit.

Frosty's slid by outside as I reached over to pop his mess for attempting cussing, its polka-dotted walls talking about Last Chance! Funyuns! Stop and make old Mr. Frosty rich! Old Frosty used to try to talk trash to my sister but he had one of those bulging-out waists old men get like the barber my daddy took us to who pressed his slope up against you when he was cutting your hair. Frosty wore pants shaped like the wide-open bell of a tuba. Carter wanted a trumpet. He was saving for one. We picked bottles from ditches in the after-noons. Carter had maybe half a trumpet in a coin jar hid un-der his dresser. Maybe Carter had took his trumpet money and paid my daddy for the haircut and my daddy had let him go and he was walking up the road almost to 692. Maybe I ought to of turned around. I couldn't take Tank's wailing for the next however many years until he got grown enough for me to leave him and not feel bad. I left Carter with his earlobe snipped off. I saw when Daddy did it, I saw the pink flesh hit Carter's shoulder and bounce and then I lost track of it when it landed in the carpet of blond hair spread out across the warped porch boards.

"Hey wait, stop," said Tank. He turned around and stared at Frosty's as if turning around and staring would slow the truck down. I had all the windows rolled down to sift out the pee smell. My head was half out the window like when people vehicle their dogs. Dogs don't want to be vehicled, you can tell by the way they stick their heads out the windows. A dog would prefer to chase a chicken, not cruise out to Little Pep to gawk at cheerleaders. I stuck my head farther out the window doggy-style. Pee smell rolling over the fields in a cloud. Mexicans pulled cukes in the fields. We passed by them and the pee smell rolled out in a cloud and I felt sorry for them Mexicans.

"Where we going where we going where we going?" said Tank.

Out the window into the wind I howled, "Where we going where we going where we going?"

Up 692 a ways was a fishpond with some nasty catfish and a trailer park which the bus we rode to school would not stop at because once someone shot out the windows (somebody said later it was a woman who didn't want her kids coming home and interrupting the stories she liked to look at after lunch) and then, a little off the road and upside a ravine, a chicken house belonged to Luby Dudley, owner of Appliance Town. The chicken house was filled with Luby's used refrigerators, freezers, stoves, televisions.

At Luby Dudley's Appliance Town chicken house I parked the truck on an overgrown two-track leading to the ravine. People dumped their shit down that ravine. It's just something about a ravine makes you want to dump shit down it. Perhaps peculiar to the coastal plain from which I and my brothers and potty-mouthed sister derive but perhaps maybe not, this habit of I-see-a-ravine, let's-dump-some-shit-down-it. Maybe it is in fact a habit of rural folk everywhere, there being no monster-armed trash trucks roving like they do up in Trent. Often you have to drive many miles in order to dispose of your waste. A ravine starts to looking real good after ten miles cooped up in a car with some humming-to-high-heaven garbage.

Allow me a long-winded example of the country dweller's love of ravines. My mother's mother was one pickle-making fool. She thought nothing of spending her weekend putting up seventy-five jars of pickles. Once fateful Friday I believe it was eight, nine months ago, my mama took us over to our grandparents' house so she could go away for the weekend. This particular weekend my mother when we asked her where she was going to be staying at said the Sanitary Restaurant in Bulkhead which had the best hush puppies she knew of. It sounded like a lie even to Tank.

"Mama, Mama, hold up, you're spending the night in the restaurant?" he asked her.

"If it's hot I'm sleeping in the walk-in freezer," she said.

We were let out of the truck at my grandmother's house, my sister carrying her *Beauty and the Beast* suitcase leftover from when she was the only child and got what she wanted, me and my brothers slumping under school backpacks bulky with underpants and Q-tips and army men. I was halfway to the house when my mama called me back to the car.

"Why are you walking like that?" she said to me.

"Like what?"

She sighed what my daddy called her Sigh of Royalty. She was beautiful in the afternoon sun, her brown hair thickened by driving open-windowed down dusty Moody Loop. She was so pretty she could pull off riding around in my daddy's pickup. We could not stay with him because he'd gone off. She'd herded us out of there fast as she could, told me to pack for Carter and Tank, ordered Angie to get her act together. Then she let us out at her parents' farmhouse and called me back and sighed her royal sigh.

"Walking like how?" I said.

And my mama, so beautiful with the dusty wind-ruffled hair, behind the wheel of the very pickup me and Tank would employ as our escape vehicle, said, "Like you're a puppet with half your dangling strings broke."

I just shrugged and rested my chin on the slot where the window disappeared on down into the door. My head half in, I studied her outfit, noticing for the first time how she had

taken some care dressing when the rest of us were wearing
whatever we always got caught in when my mama herded us
off, dirty-kneed jeans and Stretch & Sew striped shirts my
mama made herself with the oversized neck holes, in Tank's
case old pee-stained underpants, and yet wasn't it odd that
she herself was got up in a jean jacket, a flowery dress, some
cowgirl boots?

And all the way to Bulkhead for a weekend just for some
hush puppies?

"Get in here for a second," she said, patting the seat next
to her.

"You take good care of your brothers," she said when I
climbed in.

"Angie last time I checked the birth records was older
than me."

"Angela is Angela," she said. "She lacks patience. She
does not have your heart."

"She's got a mouth on her, though."

My mama laughed. "Don't pay any attention to her mouth.
Just take care of your brothers and hold your shoulders up."

"When you coming back on Sunday?" I asked her. I
wanted to say the word "Sunday" because it had happened
before, this dropping us off at my grandparents for a so-called
weekend that started out the weekend but dipped big-time
into the week. I hated to hear she was leaving us at all, much
less for the weekend which she must of gotten mixed up with
the week. Sunday Sunday Sunday say it again so she'll hear
you say it Sunday.

Instead she answered a question I never asked her. As she talked she looked out the window at the woods behind the house she grew up in, as if these woods held old, favored shadows, or dreams of someplace wider. I knew she was speaking to me but not to me too.

"I just want a stretch of days where I know exactly what's going to happen next. He's worth it, I love him still, I love all y'all but it's just so hard not knowing whether he'll be there when I get home from work. And even if he's there half the time he's not there. I just need some time. They'll take good care of ya'll. Not that he wouldn't."

She turned her head away from those woods, toward me. "He's not going to hurt any of you, you know that. He's not capable of that. He loves you all just the same whether he's off or on, it's just, well, he's sick's what it is, baby. You know that. That's why I brought y'all up here to stay awhile. It'll be better for everybody, you'll see."

"What time on Sunday, though?"

"Go on now," she said. "Mama said she's got something she needs y'all's help with," she said.

"See you Sunday," I said.

I got out of the truck and went back to walking broke-string puppet but she slapped that truck in gear and was gone.

Inside my grandmother immediately put us to work making pickles. But then she discovered something wrong with the cukes, I forgot what, but the whole batch was bad. Ceremoniously did she call out for my grandfather. He came out of a back dark bedroom blinking from a deep-down nap.

"Take these children and dump these pickles down a ravine."

He looked at her like what the hell's wrong with them. She put her hands on her hips, indignant. Seemed like they'd been married too long to trust words. Or maybe they'd used up their allotment and were down to threadbare gestures. The only word that seemed to matter was "ravine." My grandfather was wore out from years of baking under the sun in his tobacco and soybean fields but he perked up a little at the mention of the magic word.

"Hot damn, I get to go looking a ravine to dump some pickles in," said my sister under her foul mouthed breath. We loaded the smelly half-pickled cukes in the pickup and lit out for the ravine. He made all four of us ride in the cab so we wouldn't get clobbered by pickle jars. My smart-assed sister kept right on ribbing my granddaddy.

"How come we got to dump them down a ravine? There's some sweet-looking woods right there," she said, pointing to the trees flashing by the pickup. My grandfather lit a Lucky Strike and fingered a flake of tobacco on his tongue, his only acknowledgment of her comments. My sister kept right on, though, and I had the idea that this would be her way with the world, with men particularly: She would wear them down with her questions. Slap them around with words. Mostly foul ones. We kept circling the county looking a ravine. "Don't you even know where one's at?" said my sister. She spit out the "at." What she meant was, What kind of laconic, born-and-bred-down No Head Bottom Road old turkey-necked man are you anyway? You'd think he was from Newark, New Jersey, the way he could not put his fingers on the exact location of a ravine.

Turned out he was looking for just the right one. I admit I admired his perseverance. Wouldn't any ravine do for this batch of spoiled pickles. He had an audience also. What would we think of him if he'd of dragged us to a ravine any fool could find, one strewed with old shirts and bottles and plastic diapers and a couple of stoves half-slid down the mud-slick plummet? I sensed he cared what me and my brothers thought, less so my smart-assed, why-won't-any-old-woods-do sister.

Finally on a dirt road down near Ivanhoe he slammed on the brakes, jerked his turkey neck around, threw his arm up along the seat behind us, bobbed his Lucky between his teeth, and floored the truck. We fishtailed to the side of the road, fell out to check the ravine. Pure virgin, deep as a well, not one iota of previous trash. I confess it touched that part of me craved basement, attic, crawl space. I wondered did I inherit this from the old ravine locator, who I vowed to pay more attention to from that point on, though I never did imagine myself or my brothers or sisters living with him or my grandmama who I don't think were ever informed of my mama's plans to let us stay with them awhile or if they were did not seem to know how to deal with three smelly boys and a foul-mouthed smart-assed girl. It was like Ringling Brothers had detoured down No Head Bottom Road and pulled up in their drive and unleashed half their wildest animals in my grandparents' front yard with nothing but a tip of some truck driver's hats.

My granddaddy let us do right much what we wanted. For instance that day at the ravine, we boys got to bomb the pickle jars off the trees. My granddaddy went off to pee and while he was gone my sister stole two of his Luckys, which of course he noticed, being the sort to keep track of what all he'd smoked by a certain time of day. But I can't claim it was my sister and her mouth and her sticky fingers led my grand-parents to let my daddy come pick us up after two weeks— maybe it was how clean and smiley my daddy was when he turned up, how he helped my grandmama with the dishes and changed the oil in my granddaddy's pickup—I won't blame any one thing on any one person, much as I would like to single somebody's guilty ass out and not have to worry about it.

Though I was starting to blame myself big-time for leaving Carter when I parked the truck alongside the ravine. Up in the shade, well out of the boiling. Tank jumped out and ran into the chicken house. You had to watch him out there or he'd climb in a refrigerator to hide and suffocate. That re-minds me, he needs to change those wet underpants, I said to myself, so starved on a day's diet of only some four-cornered Nabs and some Pop Rocks that I was talking with a vengeance to myself in the cab of the truck, just slack sitting there, listen-ing to the tick of the engine and far off Tank banging around some discarded discount appliances, unable to move due to exhaustion, fear, hunger, anger at having to be thinking about someone else's underwear. Also guilt: a pinkish dollop of flesh floated down from the boiling sky in front of the dust-streaked windshield, bouncing off pine needles, before settling in similarly colored sand. I lost my brother's earlobe. How come I never slipped the key into the ignition and left when I had the chance? I did not have to sit there all day in that boiling truck waiting on whatever evil you want to call it—for there were many names for what inhabited my father and not one of them made anything easier—to pass. Why did I not leave like my mama and my sister? Who was I to think I could win out over the kind of fate that had doomed my family since before I turned up in somebody's stomach? If only she had not named me after him.

Then it hit me how I could change my name. Up in town, Hargrove's Laundry sold work clothes on a rack out front. Stitched in red thread above cigarette pockets were all grades of names. Tank too could alter his identity. We'd even snag one for Carter. No money required as Tank could foray into Hargrove's to distract the skinny, blue-smock-wearing, bug-eyed woman behind the counter while I generously helped myself and my brothers to new identities. Doors would then open for us. We could hire ourselves out as a uniformed crew.

"Tank," I called. "Hole up, Tank, I got a good idea."

But I hadn't taken two steps toward the chicken house before I saw again that fluttering lobe. Everywhere and constant in my field of vision, steady floating like gnats or raindrops. Closed my eyes, opened them: still there.

"Tank, Tank, where you at?" I said.

Up inside that chicken house it was cool and bluely shadowed. Sometimes we napped in the sand like dogs despite the previous tenants, the high and likely fact that our sandy bed was well fertilized with their droppings. It was a peaceful place in our lives, the upside-the-ravine, dead-appliance chicken house. But that day it didn't feel right. It smelled hellish, of decayed chickenshit and pee-stiff underpants. I yelled Tank's name until it echoed tinny off the half acre of discarded appliances. All I wanted was a shirt declaring my new name stitched over my heart. In the elevator of my mother's hotel I stood toward the back among the elegantly dressed residents when she entered. She half-turned to look at me as we rose up through the floors. Joel Junior? she asked. The rest of the elevator half-turned too to hear my name. I counted to three, thumped the cursive crowning my heart, and said, No, ma'am, the name is Thaddeus.

"Thaddeus," I yelled. My stomach and I had come to the end of the Pop Rocks, the four-cornered Nabs. The Fig Newtons and ginger ale my mother had offered had long since been siphoned off by the boiling sun. Also expired: any remaining patience I had as big-brother/mother/father all rolled into one. I would not allow myself to think about what might have actually happened to Carter after we left. If I thought about it with eyes closed I saw Carter still belted to the chair and my daddy wielding still his bloody scissor. I loved my daddy, he was a good man. He just did what the voices told him to. He was just following directions.

I found Tank curled asleep in a bathtub. He had folded himself in there like a shirt tucked clean in a drawer. But then I got close enough to smell him.

I shook him awake. He gave me his cross face and fell right back asleep. I remembered when I was his age, how I hated for anyone to wake me up. I hardly ever cried, my mama told me. Not like Carter and Tank, who were always wailing, still are, Tank anyway, he was fixing to wail when I had to snatch his underpants off him. I didn't know where I could get him another pair, especially not ones with Scooby-Doo on them, his favorite. I didn't know where I could wash the ones he had on either. There was a soapsudsy creek called the Cat Tail up 692 in Trent but you could lose your toe to its splash. It stunk up the whole bottom down by the jail, the library and liquor store. Occasionally you'd see the haz-mat crew standing around down there in their space suits. Again I shook him awake and again he shifted and shot me his cross face and fell right back asleep. I didn't know what to do with him or what to do with me either. We couldn't go back home. We couldn't go see Sheriff Deputy Rex. He would put us in foster hell. I imagined he'd dearly love to split us up. I was not about to lose Tank that way. I'd soon leave him side of the road in his dirty underwear or asleep in a tub wearing his cross face.

My grumbling stomach reminded me of how sometimes fat Frosty took pity on us when word reached him that my daddy had gone off again and he'd give us hot dogs apiece and once a Nutty Buddy to split. One thing, when I get old enough I'm not going to share jack shit. I am here to tell you that even if a sweet girl comes up to me and asks me to share her whatever I am going to tell her I'd rather do without.

I shook him awake again and his red face rose up out of the tub, his cheeks creased by the sticks and leaves blanketing the bottom. Not once have I ever mentioned to someone not kin to me by blood and by that I mean brother, sister, or mother my daddy's troubles. Not even to Sheriff Deputy Rex when he comes to get us and asks me straight questions. I didn't know what else to do though. We had to eat. Also if I was going to leave Carter behind because I was so good at love then I couldn't just keep running without telling some body about that lobe I saw falling whatever I looked at, wherever I went. I was not going to walk through this world seeing eyes shut or closed that severed piece of falling pink.

I picked him up finally and toted him rag doll and sweaty over to the truck. I laid him across the seat. He didn't even wake when I took off his shorts and then his Scooby-Doos. I put his shorts back on him and stuffed the balled-up underpants under the seat and opened the windows wide and scooted up in the driver's seat. Tank went right on sleeping, do not disturb.

Old Frosty from behind the counter said when I walked in, "Boy, your daddy know you driving his vehicle?"

Same old semicircle of men sat around gumming tobacco and listening to him bitch. The whole place smelled fried. Usually it made me gag, that trapped odor of a thousand sausage biscuits, but I was so dang hungry that Frosty's smelled like heaven.

"Mr. Frosty can I talk to you back there?" I said, pointing toward the drink coolers. They were humming and oozing spillage onto the sloping concrete floors. It was dark and smellier in the corner but I did not want the semicircle listening to my business.

"What the hell for?" asked Frosty.

"For about one minute of your time."

"I'm a busy man," lied that too-fat-to-push-through-the-slot-behind-the-register, has-to-turn-sideways-and-grunt-to-get-out fool.

"Say what it is you want, ain't nobody listening to you."

Standing there in Frosty's, the semicircle hanging on my silence, I thought college was not such a bad idea after all. I wondered if the full-time study of maps would possibly allow me enough free time to pursue other interests such as kickboxing. In terms of giving back to the community I felt that I would be a decent volunteer fireman.

Tank's favorite book was *Dumbo*. He liked to look at the picture where the elephant's up in the tower and the firemen are urging him to jump onto a tiny trampoline. I believe if I'm not mistaken it's right before Dumbo discovers his dumb-ass can fly. We read the same page over and over and every time Tank urges Dumbo to go ahead, go for it, jump!

"Please, Mr. Frosty," I said, "it won't take but two minutes."

"His real name ain't really Frosty," said one of the tobacco gummers.

"That boy don't give a spit what my real name is," said Frosty. He got up and hoisted the belt on his tuba pants, which had slid down past his gut. He pushed his belly side-ways through the slot. We all watched him do it like it was a ball game replayed in slow motion on an un-golf-clubbed TV.

"What?" he said, patting sweat off his forehead. I walked back to the coolers and he followed, asking, "What? What?"

"It's my daddy."

"That crazy fucker gone off again?"

The concrete sloped toward a drain. I stood in something sticky. My feet made ripping noises when I tried to lift them. I never knew what I was going to say until I said it. Before I could say anything Frosty said, "Where's Carter at?"

Then this half-asleep, hoarse dwarf voice goes, "My daddy stuffed bananas down Carter's throat. He ain't peeled them. Then he tied him up with belts and cut his ear off."

"You get back in the truck," I told Tank. I gave him back his own cross look. He was sweaty red from napping. He was twisting around, palming his mess like he had to pee.

"You need the bathroom, boy?" said Frosty.

"Naw, he pees his pants," I said.

Tank just stood there staring at me.

"You best not be thinking I'm going to take you," I told Tank.

"I want you to," he said in a little girly whine.

"Get your ass in there and do your business."

"I don't know where it's at."

"Goddamn," said Frosty. "Sam! Take this boy out back while I talk to his brother and make sure he don't pee all over my floor."

An overalled man ambled back shrugging. He held out his hand.

"Where's your thumb at?" said Tank.

We all looked. Sure enough it was missing.

"Don't be rude to that man. He's going to help you. Do you have to go or not?" I asked him.

"Number two too."

"This ain't math class," I said.

"Jesus Lord," said Frosty. When they were gone he said, "What's this about a banana and a ear?"

"We had to leave right quick. That's how come I'm driving the truck."

"You ain't answered the question."

"He didn't cut his ear off. He just sort of nicked it with some scissors while he was giving him a haircut."

"Well, which the hell is it? First you say you had to leave out of there quick enough to steal your daddy's vehicle. Then you tell me he was just cutting the boy's hair."

Frosty was smarter than I thought. I'd never seen him in action, I guess. Only thing I had seen him do prior was ring stuff up. If you asked him he'd give you a bag but only if you asked him and then he'd make a big deal out of licking his fat finger, reaching below the counter to extract with excruciating slowness a paper bag, flapping the thing open ceremoniously in the fly-crazy airspace above the register, loading your purchases in such a way as to suggest what a tremendous pain in the ass you were to request a bag. The entire process added another five minutes to your overall time in line and has never convinced me that beneath that gruff exterior lies hidden a keen intellect.

I was thinking, however, that perhaps there was a way to get a tank of gas out of this slow-motion fucker.

"He went off early this morning," I said. "He cut the tip off Carter's ear. We ain't had anything to eat or drink since breakfast."

Frosty let out a fat man's sigh, as if he'd been punctured and was slow-leaking.

"You wanting me to extend your daddy credit when he's fixing to be carted off to Dix Hill?"

"It was just a accident."

"I guess the law'll have to decide that. I know if I cut the tip off my boy's ear, they'd have my fat ass up in front of a judge before I could get out from behind that counter."

"My daddy's a good man," I said.

"Your daddy's crazier than a goddamn bedbug. Where's your mama at?"

I said, "All I'm saying is, he'll pay you back in a few days. He always pays up."

"She run off, that's right, I believe I heard that back here."

"The truck's almost out of gas."

"You best leave that truck here. Don't, the law will be looking you *and* your daddy."

"If you can just spot me a loaf of bread and some peanut butter and a couple Co-colas and a tank of gas so I can take Tank up to town to my daddy's sister's house I tell you what I'll come back down here and work it off."

My daddy doesn't have a sister. I wouldn't accept employment at Frosty's if I was dead starving. I'd rather steal cukes out of the fields. Bad cukes, ravine cukes, ones not even Mexicans would eat.

"I don't need no help."

"I'll sweep and mop this floor."

"My place don't need cleaning."

I questioned his standards. But, you know, everyone has their priorities.

"What about the outside?"

"What about it?"

"You need more gravel in that parking lot. It ain't nothing but mud puddle."

"You ain't strong enough to sling gravel."

"You order up a half ton and I'll have that parking lot level as a landing strip."

"If I agree to this, it's because as crazy as he is I like your daddy."

"He's a loyal customer."

"Hell, there's no such thing. They come by here when they run out of milk, but let a Food Lion open up in town and they act like they don't know my country ass."

"Maybe you ought to knock down your prices a little bit, Frosty."

"My name ain't Frosty. You get what you need and I'll order up that gravel. If your ass ain't back down here by six o'clock I'm calling the law on you, your daddy, and your foul-smelling little brother."

I didn't tell him this is exactly what I wanted him to do. I couldn't very well bring myself to call the law on my daddy but somebody needed to. I went around collecting my goods: a loaf of Merita, a jar of crunchy, some Ruffles, two big cold bottles of Co-cola. Back behind the counter, Frosty frowned and wrote it all down on his tab pad, which he kept chained to the counter. He went to lick his bag finger and I suffered through the bagging process, which lasted about three days.

"Ten dollars on number one," said Frosty.

Cheap sapsucker. Ten dollars was three-quarters of a tank.

I found Tank outside sitting on a bench sucking on a bottle of Mountain Dew. No-thumbed Sam had sprung for it. "They's cheaper out here than in yonder," Sam twanged. He had a voice like a flapping loose guitar string. Frosty was right, there's no such thing as loyalty. I thought of Carter. He ought not to of gotten out of that truck. I told him, I told him. We were just going to sing some Curtis. I had a whole repertoire lined up, had filed the order in my head like any good DJ. Up next was "Freddie's Dead," then "Move on Up." We'd end our Curtis set with "(Don't Worry) If There's a Hell below We're All Going to Go." Then I thought we'd get into some Sly. Maybe "Everybody Is a Star," "Hot Fun in the Summertime," "Dance to the Music." Those were Carter's and Tank's favorites. Myself I preferred the ones with the thumpy bass lines: "Family Affair" and especially "If You Want Me to Stay."

"If You Want Me to Stay" snaked up in my head while I was pumping the gas. I didn't realize I was singing until I looked up and saw Sam and the rest of the semicircle staring at me. They had moved out to the benches, I suspected because Frosty was in a less than stellar mood now that he had accepted credit from the son of a man who may or may not have just bodily harmed his own blood kin. He knew he wasn't going to get his money back. He must have known I wasn't coming back. "If You Want Me to Stay" was about a man and a woman but if you just let the bass line enter your spinal cord it worked for near about any situation which is why me and Carter and Tank loved some Sly Stone better than, say, Star-Spangled Banner or the hymns they played the few times our grandmother had carried us to church. I especially liked the part where Sly swears he'll be good and then gets all impatient with the woman, saying he wished he could get his message over to her right damn now which I understood completely how awful it is to want to talk to someone and you're not allowed to talk to them I guess because they don't want to talk to you.

Tank was already into the Ruffles when I got in the car. He'd dropped half of them on the seat, between the seat, on the floorboard, all down his shirt. He was cramming them in his mouth and crunching like he was being timed. I snatched the bag out of his hand and said, "Don't you know this has got to last us?"

He went to wailing. I slapped him to shut him up. All this in plain view of the semicircle, who watched us without expression or, that I could see, any exchanged words. I'm sure we were a whole lot more interesting than Frosty.

I dug another rut in the lot I won't about to fill with gravel leaving Frosty's. I was telling myself I'd see this place again even though I knew it wasn't likely. Tank was wailing still. He was so tired. The sun was going down. I pulled over by a Dumpster to make him a peanut butter sandwich. There was hardly any trash in the Dumpster, the locals favoring ravines.

He refused the sandwich. He wouldn't look at me. He was balled up by the door, arms over his head, as if I was about to pop him again.

I tried talking to him. Just sniffles in return.

Finally I tried our favorite joke. "What do McDonald's coffee and Eric Clapton have in common?"

From beneath those arms came a faint monotone and I knew he was with me for as long as I could stay. "They both of them suck without cream."

THREE

WE HAD SOME STOPS to make in town. It was a risk, me driving my daddy's pickup up and down those three or four main streets. People knew him, knew his ride. When he was up he was the uppest man around. He smiled like a television preacher. People wanted to be around him, they wanted to hear him talk his trash. They liked to hear him sing his soul music hits like "Mr. Big Stuff" which he liked to sing to all of us whenever we got too big for our britches. When I was little I used to spy on my mama and daddy when they were sitting out on the porch after supper, rocking in the porch swing, my mama's legs in my daddy's lap, my daddy pushing off the porch boards now carpeted by Carter's favorite blond hair with his mud-stained work boots or sometimes his bony white feet. It looked like an advertisement the way they laughed and talked and rubbed each other's shoulders.

Of course when he went off it was the offest off, and the advertisements for sweet porch-swing love between two people who had known each other since high school were hard to remember. Sometimes he was just snake-on-the-ground down. He moved and spoke like he was fighting his way up from a river of mud. He had come unplugged. Any room he walked in, shadows and cobwebs would drape the corners. I'd see him dragging ass and my own lights would dim and I'd hate him a little even though I loved my daddy, he was a good man.

They were fixing to close when we reached Hargrove's. It was ten till six and when I pulled up in front of the racks of work shirts out front I could see that skinny blue-smocked woman look at me like, don't you even think about coming in here at no ten till. It is my personal opinion that the very skinny are much meaner than the grossly overweight. Meanness is what has burned the fat off their bones. In my home-town of Trent, North Carolina, it seemed everyone was either too big or skinny-mean. There wasn't any in between now that my mama had left. High up in some hotel, lighting cigarettes off emergency-only candles.

I said to Tank, "Go in there and tell that woman you got to go."

"Naw, I just went."

"I'll give you this Coke if you go again."

Tank discovered a Ruffle in a fold of his camping britches. He favored those pants because they had zippers on the pockets and a hammer hook. You could not take them off of him. He popped the chip in his mouth quick and looked at me to see if I'd say anything.

"I ain't got to go."

"Yes you do. See that woman?"

"That blue woman? She's mean as hell."

"No, she's not. She's a blue angel. Go in there and tell her you need to use her bathroom. Get her to take you to it. It's all the way in the back. Don't get your hand caught in one of those shirt-hauling machines."

His eyes bugged. He raised up in the seat, tucked his knees beneath him to get some elevation.

"They got shirt haulers in there?" Tank loved a conveyor belt.

"Get in there, you can see it up close."

Tank stared. Then he unfolded his legs out from under him.

"Naw," he said. "I ain't got to go."

I guess I'd had enough. I leaned across and opened his door and pushed him the hell out. A black woman with blue high heels and a church hat saw the whole thing. She shook her head at me and came over to see was Tank okay.

"Is that your daddy?" I heard her ask him.

"Hell no," said Tank. He was brushing himself off. Ruffle dust sifting off him in the dusky light.

"Who is that then?"

"Tell Miss Big Stuff none of her bidness, she's never gonna win my love," I said to the dash of my daddy's truck.

I heard Tank say, "I'm okay, it's okay."

"Tell her thank you," I said a little louder. She looked over to see me mouthing something. I knew she thought I was talking some kind of racist trash. She shook her head like *I done tried my best, I could of kept on walking* and went on up the street.

I watched Tank tell the blue-smocked lady he had to go. I saw the disgust in her face. She looked at me and asked him a question. He didn't even turn around. He palmed his mess and did his I-got-to-go dance. She had to lead him back there or else he was liable to get caught up in all that machinery. While they were gone I went through the shirts. I got six, a change for each of us. An Ed, a Larry, a Roman, a Mario, a James, a Cliff. Williams Grading, PCE Industries, Merita, Maola Milk, Johnson Distributing, Exxon. They were all too big and stiff with starch but I didn't have time to be trying mess on.

The blue-smocked woman brought Tank out to the truck. I saw her coming just in time to push the shirts up under the seat.

"This ain't no public restroom, you know."

"I'm sorry," I said. "It's just he had to go and there wasn't anywhere else to stop."

She looked up and down the street, then back to me. "Does this look like the only store on this street to you?"

I said, "We really do appreciate it."

"Y'all've been in here before asking to use the facilities, I recognize y'all."

Tank was in the truck now. He was rooting around on the floorboard. He bent over and pulled up Ed from PCE Industries.

"Hey, what's this?" he said.

I shoved my daddy's pickup in gear and stomped on it. In the rearview the blue-smocked woman pointed a finger at the truck. I could see her bony face tighten, could see her mouth open and mean skinny words spill out.

"Goddamn, Tank, what'd you do that for?"

"What?" said Tank. He was pulling out all the shirts and looking them over.

"We needed some clothes."

"You stold these?"

"I borrowed them."

"You're going to bring them back?"

"Once I wash them."

"They ain't clean?"

"Shut up, will you?"

"Give me my Coke and I will."

I reached under the seat and pulled out the Coke. It was shook up from my wild driving. Coke shot all over the cab when he opened it. I could not keep the boy. I knew it then, tearing through the streets of town, half-stopping at lights and signs, pulling all the bad traffic moves will get you caught and it all just common sense, I'd never taken a driving lesson in my life but I'd been riding in a car since I could remember. Same with taking care of my little brothers. Wasn't like I took lessons or read books on the subject. Some things I was born okay at. Other things came so slow or not at all. Other people. Either I'm like, Mr. Big Stuff, who do you think you are, or I'm at your mercy.

"Are some policemen after us?" asked Tank.

We were on backstreets by then, behind the armory.

"No."

"Shoot," said Tank.

"You better hope they don't come after us."

"Will they put us in the jailhouse?"

"Worse."

"What's worse than jail?"

"You know what a foster home is?"

"Yes," he mumbled.

"What is it then?"

"I don't know."

"I figured. It's when they take you away from your family and put you with some complete strangers and they pay those strangers to keep you."

"How's that worse than jail? Are there bars on the windows?"

"The strangers just keep the money and you don't get squat."

"How do you know so much about it?"

"I just know things."

"You don't know about jail. You never been in jail."

"I ain't planning on finding out either. Which means we got to get out of here."

"How about Cart? Can't he come?"

I looked over at Tank. His camping britches had dried Coke stains all over them. He was so sweetly dumb to this world.

"Carter's going to stay with Daddy awhile, Tank."

"I want to stay with Daddy."

"Sorry, buddy."

"Daddy cut Cart."

"That was a accident."

"He pushed bananas in his mouth."

"Daddy's sick."

"What's wrong with him?"

I had come to the house I was searching for. It belonged to the parents of this girl named Carla, the only known close personal friend of our sister, Angela. Carla was this pouty, slutty eye-shadowed girl who never seemed to notice me because I was three years younger, without a car or anything else to offer her. She would know, if anyone knew, where my sister was. I wasn't looking for my sister. I was looking for my mama, and I wanted my sister to tell me where she was.

"What's wrong with him?" Tank said again.

"He's sick," I said again. I pulled onto the shoulder a little past Carla's parent's place. Carla stayed around back in a converted garage. She was too wild to stay in the house. I knew all this because Angie used to tell me stories about Carla all the time. She'd figured out I was interested. One day she would go on and on about Carla and her wildness and the next day if I asked about Carla she would say, What do you care, Carla don't even know who you are, if she does know it's only because of me, you're out of your league, Junior, on and on until Carter, who always stuck close to Angie when she was around the house, would start laughing at me.

"What kind of sick?"

I was about to smack his broken-record ass. I said, "Do you want to see your mama?" I never should have asked him if he wanted to see his mama. But I just wanted him to shut the hell up.

"Yes," came his little up-under-a-blanket, about-to-cry voice.

"Well, shut the hell up then and come with me and don't say nothing."

I figured Carla would be more likely to tell the truth if she saw Tank in his Coke-stained camping britches.

"I'm about frozen," he said, so I wrapped him up in Ed from PCE Industries. It came down to his knees. He ran his fingers over the red-threaded letters and said, "What does this say?"

I shook my finger in his face. "What did I tell you?"

He reached for my hand while we waited at the door. A boy answered it. I'd seen him around school. He was weaving and squinting. Big clouds of cigarette smoke sucked out of the slivered door.

"What?"

"Is Carla here?"

"What do you want with her?"

"To ask her a question."

This set him off. He had a machine-gun laugh. I knew he was high, laughing semiautomatically at nothing at all.

Carla came to the door. She stared at me like I was out of place in time. Her shirt was hanging off her shoulder, exposing a sadly white and raggedy bra strap. She was carrying a beach ball on her hip like it was her baby.

"Who are you?"

"I'm Angela's brother."

"Me too," said Tank. He was eyeing that beach ball.

"Oh hey, Tank," she said. My sister's friends loved Tank. They used to follow him around and listen to him say crazy-to-them-but-normal-to-him Tank things. He'd rub dirt on the back of a dog and when they asked him why he'd say, They like to roll in it, I'm only helping, which made sense to them because they were high and sense to Tank because he was Tank.

"Well, what?"

"I need to find Angela."

"Why you asking me?"

"You're the only one I can ask."

"Well, you asked," she said, tossing the ball over our heads and pushing the door closed.

Tank started wailing. I was about to smack him but the door slivered open again and she said, "Jesus Christ, what did I say? Did you want the ball?"

"I don't want any dumb ball, I want Angie," wailed Tank.

Good work, Tank, I nearly said.

Carla kneeled down and hugged him. She nearly fell over, she was so wacked. Tank held on to her neck but I could tell he wasn't happy. Crafty little fucker.

"I'm so sorry, Tank," said Carla. She was crying on his

shoulder. Her eye shadow was melting. Suddenly some other mood hit her and she sniffled and rubbed her eyes dry and straightened Tank's shirt and said, "Hey, cool shirt, Tank."

"Will you tell us where she is?" said Tank.

Carla stood up. She looked at me and said, "If you fucking tell her I told you, man, I'll have you killed."

Yeah, okay, right, I wanted to say. There was nothing sadder to me than a seventeen-year-old girl talking street tough with her worn-out bra strap exposed. But I swore to her I'd never tell, even though Angela would know as soon as I showed up who ratted her out

"She's down at Bottomsail," said Carla. "She's working at the Breezeby, waiting tables. At least she was last weekend. I went down there to see her. She lives with this guy named Termite. He's not a real big guy," she said, and then she burst out laughing and Tank smiled at her and I grabbed Tank by the oversized work shirt and dragged him back to the truck. Inside I buckled him in and said, "Thanks, Tank."

"For what?"

"For getting her to tell us."

"She would of told you," he said.

So sweetly trusting dumb. I thought, I can't leave him, but I also thought, Neither can I keep him.

Bottomsail Beach was only forty-five miles away, but I had not a clue how to get there. I'd never driven farther than Moody Loop. I'd never driven in town and I'd never driven after dark. Cars had their lights on and the night eyes of cats blinked up from the ditches. I drove with my hands tight on the wheel to the Piggly Wiggly parking lot, where I parked behind the Dumpsters.

"What are we doing?" asked Tank. "I don't have to go."

I reached past him, slapped open the glove compartment, fished out a worn map. Daddy loved a map. He would spread them out on his lap and read them like some men read the classifieds. This one had routes inked along the spindly roads of the coastal plain, which was filled with big blue ovals signaling lakes and wavy marks telling you where the swamps were. Because of all the water you had to go around your thumb to get to your ass down here, Daddy used to say. But it struck me, looking at the map, trying to find some backroads to Bottomsail which would not be crawling with cops and would not be hard to navigate in the blackness, that he was always going around his thumb to get to his ass because some voice in his head said turn left or right or turn around and go home or lie down in the hammock and sing "Superstition" by Little Stevie Wonder or whatever it was the voices told him to do.

I thought about asking Tank to help me navigate but when I looked at him he was sneaking his hands up and down the seat cushions in search of some stray Ruffles. He'd chugged his whole bottle of Coke. He'd be up all night, peeing. Which reminded me, he needed some underpants. It was too much. I made him a peanut butter sandwich by the streetlight, ripped off the crust like he liked. I rationed him a sip of my Coke for every fifty chews. Counting would keep him busy.

I could not have that boy chattering and filing his wild blue yonder supremely unanswerable questions when I was trying to negotiate the strange dark countryside.

On the road I started singing "Mr. Big Stuff." "Who do you think you are?" I sang to myself driving my daddy's truck down the nighttime streets.

"Daddy sings that song," said Tank.

"I know. He taught me it."

"Wonder what they're doing now."

I started to make something up. It seemed like that was my job, to tell reassuring lies. But Tank was worth more than a Band-Aid lie. Plus he was too smart for it. He'd come right back at me if I was to put him off with a patch.

"I don't know," I said.

"I bet Daddy made Carter sweep up all that hair."

"I bet so."

We were only five miles out of town. The shoulders of the road steamed. Tank's innocent blather cut through me like the headlights diced the swamp-foggy dusk. I could have turned back. I could have done the right thing, by law at least.

But I looked over and caught Tank sneaking sips of my Coke. The right thing by law of the truck was to belt his sneaky ass.

Tank sat there pouting after I popped him. He wouldn't talk. He wouldn't sing. I could have switched on the radio but I did not need the distraction. He slumped there chewing his peanut butter sandwich. Finally he fell asleep against the door. We passed through Chinquapin and Holly Springs and crossed 17 and reached the big ribbed bridge over the sound. The tires of the truck sang loudly and the body shimmied and I held on terrified to the wheel. From the highest hump of the bridge I saw all the island lit up with night lights, the motels with their neon signs, the fishing piers strung out into the black old ocean, a Ferris wheel spinning. I slapped Tank on the shoulder. He made his whining don't-mess-with-me, I'm-asleep noise: unnh.

"Wake up and look at this Tank."

He rocked up so violently I nearly lost my grip on the steering wheel.

"Dog," he said. "Where we at?"

"Bottomsail Beach."

"Mama's here?"

"No, buddy."

"There's a roller coaster," he said, stabbing his finger toward the Ferris wheel.

"That's a Ferris wheel."

"Naw it ain't."

"Okay, Tank."

"Where's the ocean?"

"See those lights," I said, pointing to the pier. "That's a fishing pier. It's built out over the water."

"Can we go down on it?"

"Okay," I said. I didn't know where the Breezeby was. I'd need some time to figure out what to say to her, what to say to Tank. I knew she wouldn't want to take him. I knew he wouldn't want to stay with her either.

The parking lot of the Jolly Roger Pier was filled with beat pickups just like my daddy's. Many of them sagged with crusty old campers. Between them in lawn chairs sat old fishwives wrapped in blankets. It was chilly in the ocean breeze. I grabbed Mario from Johnson Distributing for myself and Larry from Merita to wrap around Tank in case he got cold on the pier.

Out on the pier the wind whipped our too-big shirts into flappy capes. A storm had just passed and the pier fishermen had layered themselves puffy to guard against wind and bait slime. Though it was only eight or nine o'clock at night we stepped over snoring lumps in greasy sleeping bags. Tank stared openmouthed at a coveralled man hunched over the railing eating cereal out of the box.

"Can we sleep out here, Joel Junior?"

I was thinking how good it was to be out of that truck. We had been in that truck for what seemed like a holiday weekend. I got the boys' breakfast and then Daddy went off right soon after and we had stayed in that truck until late afternoon. I was thinking about Carter, was he hurt bad or lying on the floor with a Band-Aid on his ear listening to *Goat's Head Soup* with my daddy, singing the words to "Hide Your Love" which was my favorite song on there though my daddy liked the one called "Coming Down Again" and Carter and Tank were partial to Starfucker though they weren't allowed to sing the words.

"We'll see," I said. I realized after these two words had come out of my mouth that I could learn how to be somebody's daddy. Defer every question they ask and hope like hell they forget to reask. But this only applied to normal kids. It didn't work on never-forget-a-half-promise Tank.

The wide planks of the pier were slick from the storm, phosphorescent from fish gut. Kids about Carter's age got to do mean things to stingrays left lying out in midpier for kids to do mean things to. These tortures were slow and cruel and drew many expressionless fishermen who sipped from bagged tallboys and watched the dismemberment soberly, as if it had been drained of all meaning from repetition but was too significant to ignore.

At the end of the pier, where the crowd thinned, me and Tank stopped to watch this old man cast. He had the magic. His reel buzzed like a fluorescent light fixture gone wrong. His casts far exceeded the armchair flicks of others which dropped limp as dangled anchors and rose in a shameful sea-weedy tangle. Me and Tank watched as the line shot toward the dark horizon. In my mind I tracked the silver hypotenuse down to where the slight hook pricked the green glass and disappeared beneath to do its sly seducing, an undercover cop posing prostitute. We watched for a half hour until the man pulled in something from far out in the dark green sea. Something big, silver, beautiful.

"A fish!" screamed Tank.

Everyone at that end of the pier laughed. I loved my little brother so much right then I scooped him up under pretense of letting him see better the big silver beautiful fish but what it was, I wanted to hold him tight. Which I did until he went to squirming and saying, Put me down, put me down.

At which point I was ready to smack him again.

Just as quickly I'd want to hug him. It was just that way with Tank, or maybe that's how it was with me and most everybody. I wanted to leave them sometimes, just go off by myself and sit and listen to whatever it was in my head, mouth the words, hum the guitar solo, but I knew how awful I was at love, I knew I'd have to just suffer through the sticky parts rather than go off by myself. It was just that other people could turn so suddenly into something like that memory that needles you out of bed in the middle of the night—say you think you might of left the toaster oven on—even when you know you turned it off and unplugged it. They aggravate you for no good reason. Take Carter. He had this way of getting away with me with just a look or a not-look, just by drumming the table when me and Tank were watching *Soul Train* or lying to Tank about something I would have lied to him about myself. People just get to me. Because I guess I let them. I sometimes envied my daddy a little when he went off, because it seemed he was at the least safe, wasn't anyone going to bother him, he was off by himself someplace nobody else could get to. Then there was my mama; she didn't even have to be like my daddy to wall herself off from everyone. I wondered how did it happen, coming from the likes of them and turning out like I turned.

The magic caster took an interest in Tank. He was nice to me because I was with Tank which was often the case when I was with Tank.

"Who you boys out here with?" he said after we'd stood there an hour watching his magic.

"Nobuddy," said Tank. He jerked his thumb at me. "Just him and me."

I kneed him to get him to shut up, let me do the talking, but Tank did not listen to my knee.

"Where's y'alls mama and daddy at?"

"My mama's gone off we don't know where to and my daddy's—"

"We're down here staying with my older sister," I said. "She works over at the Breezeby."

I had worked over close enough to Tank to grab the excess of his wind-billowed work shirt and tighten and yank it to get him to look at me. I shushed him. Fortunately the magic caster had his eyes on his lines the whole time he was talking to us. Tank nodded as he liked anything conspiratorial, even when he didn't understand it. To him it was like hide-and-seek.

"She working right now?"

"She's with her boyfriend."

"Told y'all take a walk?"

"It's not but one room," I said.

"Y'all had anything to eat?"

"We're good," I said.

"I'm not, I'm about starving," said Tank. That was the thing about hide-and-seek, it never lasted very long.

"You know how to tell if a fish is biting?" the pier fisherman asked me.

"Yes, sir," I lied.

"Watch my poles while I run inside then."

Thankfully nothing bit until magic caster returned with bags of chips, sausage biscuits, and corn dogs. For dessert he had bought orange pushups which by the time we got to them dripped all over Larry from Merita and Mario from Johnson Distributing. He said he was going to stay out there all night long and when I said my sister told us not to come home he asked us to watch the poles again and went to his truck and got us some sleeping bags. I was a little worried Tank would roll off into the ocean — I'd spent many a night with him in our bed at home when he got scared and came and climbed in with me and I knew what a roller he was — but the magic caster must have sensed my worry as he said he'd be right there with us, if he had to go to the bathroom he'd hang it off the side. We bedded down on the hard smelly slats and listened to the ocean waving and sucking itself back in. Wood creaked as the pier swayed. Tank slept like the baby he was. I went in and out of it but I would not have slept anywhere in the world that night as tired and worried as I was.

In the morning the magic caster bought us juice and some donuts. He let Tank drink some of his coffee which Tank pronounced sweet as pie. Tank had to go to the bathroom so I took him down under the pier where we both peed against the pilings and then Tank took off running wild down the beach, laughing, and I loved him again and took off after him, yelling, "Hey now, hold up, Mr. Big Stuff, just who do you think you are?"

FOUR

WAITING FOR MY SISTER to show up at the Breezeby, we sang some Otis. My daddy sometimes when he was between off and on used to talk to us from that in-between zone. I wanted to believe the things he told us and I almost could because his eyes had not yet turned into plate-glass windows you see yourself in walking down the sidewalk. Once my daddy told us that he happened to be in Madison, Wisconsin, the day that Otis Redding's plane crashed in a nearby lake and soon as word reached him he hopped in his truck and drove out there and hired some old boy fishing in a fourteen-foot Ouachita with a twenty-horse Evinrude to motor him out to where the plane disappeared beneath the icy water. He didn't even bother putting on any frogman suit because, he said, time was of the essence. He's the one dove down and pulled Otis from the wreckage of wrong plane, wrong time. The other passengers, still belted in the seats, swayed in the murky water like they were grooving to a slow jam on the radio. The plane had lost part of its engine but the cabin was intact except some loose sheet music bobbing about like fish. My daddy grabbed a page and studied the notes. Surely it was a new song Otis was working on. He hadn't written it down though, it was in his head and such sudden death unleashed it on paper, ticking off the unsaid and unfinished thoughts before they were lost to the world forever. It's not the things you say that make you brilliant, it's the things you think that you can't say, my daddy told us. They say a man only uses a fraction of his brain, well, surely he only uses a few words. That's why I like music, it taps right into things you feel in your veins but can't just up and outright say.

"Where they at now?" Carter had asked him.

My daddy had stared at Carter like he was speaking Spanish.

"Them pages of Otis's?"

But my daddy had gone too far off to answer.

Oh but he loved some Otis. There wasn't all that many songs to learn given Otis's cut-short career and my daddy knew them all. The ones he loved best had something-another to do with a heart: "Pain in My Heart," "This Heart of Mine." Also the ones featuring the word *love*: "That's How Strong My Love Is," and "I've Been Loving You Too Long (to Stop Now)"

Tank was wanting to sing "(Sittin' on) The Dock of the Bay." I guess because we were sitting on a dock behind the Breezeby restaurant, out over the sound. I was feeling okay despite my patchy night of pier sleep and did not want to come to the chorus which no matter how okay I felt, starting in on that chorus made me feel low. In the chorus Otis basically claims nothing's going to change, everything's going to stay just like it is. The entire start-to-finish song is down-on-the-ground low but because of all that whistling people who don't know no better than to listen to the words (and Tank and them who just sing them without really *thinking* them) mistake it for a happy song. Though with songs like "Dock," it makes some sense not to listen to every word. Just let the notes fall all over you like sweet rain. Drink it down like you do a glass of water in a shadowy afternoon kitchen on a boiling day.

Tank was already to the whistling. He could not whistle worth a spit. His bad whistling was way better than Otis saying he had nothing to live for. Sometimes at home when we'd play *The Very Best of Otis Redding* and this song would come on with its water rustling in the opening notes I would let myself fall right down into it. I wanted to feel its sadness washing over me. But right then, waiting for my sister to show up at the Breezeby, I did not want any part of that need-to-feel-bad-to-feel-good low-downness.

My daddy used to say that when Otis bring in that song to record his people looked at him like he was gone off. They were looking hits, said my daddy, they were wanting another "I've Been Loving You Too Long" or "Try a Little Tenderness." What other song do you know with any whistling in it but the old theme from Andy of Mayberry? But Otis kept after them, said my daddy, and after he died it became his signature hit. My daddy knew everything there was to know about Otis Redding. He knew the name of the street he was born on in Macon, Georgia. He claimed to have once laid eyes on Otis's widow in a club in Alpharetta, Georgia. He knew who was twiddling the knobs on those Stax/Volt classics, what session men played on what single. Otis wrote "Dock" in a houseboat in Sausalito, California, he told us one time.

You want to *whistle?* I imagine Otis's producers said to him when he brung in "Dock of the Bay." I listened to Tank's off-key, barely recognizable-as-Otis warbling and imagined myself as Otis, holding on to what felt right, winning over the world in the end.

We were sitting on the dock when I saw my sister Angela picking her way barefoot through a sandy back lot filled with sandspurs and oyster shells. She was smoking with her head down, carrying her shoes in one hand. A very strange thing had happened since I'd seen her last: she'd turned beautiful. She looked like my mama but younger and thinner. She was wearing a white waitress uniform with pockets in front of her skirt for ticket books. Both pockets bulged with boxes of cigarettes. She had her hair pulled back in a ponytail. I'd never seen her hair any way other than stringy in her face. Because my sister has always known how to get what she wants out of boys she stayed tomboyish for as long as she could. At the last possible second—about the time the pack of boys who followed her through the woods to forts made out of fallen pines and stolen sheet metal started to like girls in general, girly ones in particular—she switched over, started hanging around with slutty Carla, squeezed herself into too-tight hip-huggers and halters. She has always had excellent timing, my sister.

I did not want Tank to see her because I wanted to surprise her. I knew if she saw us outside her job she'd just open her foul mouth and let fly the filth. So I pointed to the end of the dock.

"Looks like a shark out there in the sound," I said.

I kept him distracted for a good hour. It got on toward lunch. At least she'd have to feed us.

"Come on," I said, tugging him away from the water, into the Breezeby.

"Why do they call it a sound?" said Tank.

"Because it doesn't make one."

"Why don't they call it what it is instead of what it ain't?"

"We call you Tank and you're not one."

This stumped him at least enough to come along with me.

I stopped him in the foyer by the gumball machines and the newspaper racks. He stared at the retard candy. My sister used to tell him when he began to beg and whine for quarters that contrary to popular belief the money did not go to retards but in fact the candy would turn whoever bought it into a retard. Not that this stopped him from begging for a quarter every time we passed a machine.

"Look, Tank," I said, "Angie's in there . . ."

"Where?" he said, pushing his face against the plate glass.

I grabbed him by his floppy work shirt which came to his

knees and was filthy. Mine was dirty too. Also too big. We were what my always putting up some pickles grandmother used to call a blessed sight.

"Hey, listen," I said. "I'm not through with that sentence. Angie's in there and I know you haven't seen her in a while and all but I don't want you screaming out her name when you see her like you did that fish on the pier last night."

"I didn't know any fish's name."

"You know what I mean."

"No I don't."

I decided to switch to threats. They worked better than reasoning.

"Are you hungry?"

"Yes."

"If you want to eat, don't say nothing until I tell you to."

I asked the hostess if we could sit in Angela's section. She was an older, teased-haired, sun-basted local, tough as a live oak. I saw something in her eyes, a hazard flashing at the mention of my sister's name. Angie was in trouble. This neither surprised nor bothered me. She was the one couldn't take it so she up and left.

We sat in a booth overlooking the sound. Tank could barely contain himself. He slid maniacally back and forth along the Naugahyde seat, playing with a stack of sugar packages.

She made us wait. This made me smile, but it made me mad too.

Then she was standing above us with her pad. "Have y'all decided?"

I saw it coming, Tank bursting into his biggest tears.

"Oh God, Tank," she said, her mouth tightening, throwing her words like a ventriloquist. It was the softest I'd ever heard her talk. "Just hold on, baby," she said. "Soon's I get off work we can talk all you want. Stop crying, okay?"

I thought I saw her eyes grow wet, but maybe it was just the sun hovering over the water, reflected in her glassy eyes.

She said to me, under her breath, "They're watching me today. I'm about to get my ass fired. This is all I need. You got any money?"

"Well, no," I said, smiling.

She fake-waitress smiled back. "You slimy fucker," she said. "What's up with those shirts y'all got on?"

"Joel Junior stold them from a rack while I made a lady take me to the bathroom," said Tank.

"Attaboy," she said to me. "Where's Carter?"

Tank looked at me before he spoke. He remembered. Attaboy. Angie looked from Tank to me and repeated her question.

"He's with your father."

"He's yours too," said Tank.

She was staring at me, trying to see in the expression I wasn't about to give her just how bad it had gotten. I must have given her something. She wrote on her pad and disappeared, returned with a basket of toast, glasses of juice, then soon after platters of pancakes with sides of bacon and small bowls of applesauce and grits.

We ate and ate. She brought the bill, reached into her

smock pocket, and pulled a twenty from behind the ticket book.

"Go get him a T-shirt, for God's sake. There's a dollar store up the block. I'll meet you out back on the dock there at five o'clock. Bring me back my change."

The Dollar Store, like all Dollar Stores, had sticky floors, flickering fluorescent lighting, disastrously disorganized shelves, a confusing floor plan, clerks who seemed to receive for a day's work no more than the namesake buck and were not happy about it, merchandise worth at most three-quarters of a dollar, piped in Carpenters' hits syrupy with strings, a vague smell of plastic and, near the break room, of chili dogs. We could have been anywhere; the only evidence that we were not an hour or two inland was a lone aisle overstocked with beach towels, umbrellas, lawn chairs, and sand toys. This aisle was clogged with children trying out the sand toys and their parents who ignored them while they tried to decide which sort of chaise lounge to waste their money on. Tank proceeded to stand at the head of the aisle and stare at the playing children with a kind of intense vacancy.

I dragged Tank to the kids clothes' aisle. He chose a purple T-shirt bearing the green gruesome likeness of an animated action figure. Since our daddy had golf-clubbed the TV we'd been out of the loop, yet Tank, I suspected, pretended familiarity with all the current shows favored among the K through 3 set just to fit in.

"Can I wear it to school?" he said before I'd even paid for it. It made me sad, his saying this. I did not want Tank to be like the rest of the world. I bought him a three-pack of Fruit of the Looms and for myself I purchased a single pair of boxers, being too old for tighty whiteys. To kill time we went next door to the surf shop and ran our hands over the smooth, curved boards. Tank was much engaged even though he likely had never seen anyone surf. The shop was staffed by surly boys in their late teens who seemed put upon, it being nice enough outside for them to paddle about on their boards despite the fact that the ocean was glass. They would alternately ignore us to talk their surfer talk ("Dude, you would not fucking believe" was how I swear three-quarters of their sentences began) or try to harass us out of there (Y'all still just looking?) Finally, more prideful than intimidated, I spent the last of my sister's money on the cheapest thing in the store, a three-pack of temporary tattoos for $3.49. Tank chose the Chinese lettering over other designs. On the back the script was translated. Tank wanted Peace and Tranquility. I wanted Strength and Good Judgment, though I would settle for the former, since I had sat too long in that truck in the boiling sun and had given up my little brother and could not therefore anymore claim to be even tolerable at the game of love. I guessed it was too late. But I wanted to believe it wasn't.

We went back to the dock. Watched the tide roll away, wasted time. Tank sensed that my mood had plummeted and lay facedown on the dock with his nose between two slats, speaking to something in the water. Occasionally an old couple would walk out on the dock from the Breezeby smelling of Captain's Platter and stare uneasily at Tank who was muttering nonstop about starfish, the superhero on his T-shirt, Carter, his mama, the dollar store, Otis Redding's plane which his daddy dove down to through the freezing green water. Listening to him lulled me into some dank, doubt-filled space. I will never find any girl to love me, I thought. I am going to spend my whole life taking care of my little brothers. I'm not ugly, I'm tall and my face is clear but what woman would want me? My dream had a hill in it and a brook and a cabin and no automobile. It did not have so far as I could see any woman waiting on me to walk home through the misty fields. That was just my dream. Then there was My Life starring Tank, who even though I'd got him finally to put on some clean Fruit of the Looms still needed a bath, and Carter which all I needed to do was get Tank squared away with Angela and I'd run back up there and pick him up. I used to think your imagination could save your life, that my dream with no woman or automobile in it and other ones like the store that hired me to count things like nail clippers and the broken-windowed ware-house I squatted in was what got me through those days when everything and everyone leaned up against me. But sitting on the dock, waiting on my sister, watching the old fried-fish-smelling couples step over Tank stretched ass up across the slats, my dreams seemed suddenly silly, proof of nothing, no kind of cure. Like Tank talking to the barnacled pilings and the shallows of the sound, I could retreat inside and be satisfied for hours. The difference was that Tank was exploring his growing inner life and I was saying, "Fuck all y'all."

My sister appeared with one of the boys from the surf shop. He had changed into jams and a T-shirt and was carrying a surfboard under his arm. They stood at the edge of the dock, clearly discussing us. The surfer boy sneered, then laughed. She did not laugh which I took as a good sign.

"This is Glenn," she said to us.

"Hey, Glenn," said Tank. All smiles, staring at the surfboard.

Glenn said, "Your name's Tank? "He turned to me and said, "What's your name? Submarine?"

Angie still did not laugh.

"Come on," Angie said, and she and Glenn took off down the pier. The way she talked to him let me know exactly what my sister was up to. Even though Glenn, with his board and his tan and his curly blond down-to-his-shoulders hair and his surf shop job was way cooler than I would ever be, I felt sorry for him. I knew Angie. I was born knowing that girl. I could hear in her voice how she was making him feel like he was the One when in fact he was nothing but the Next Fucking Rung as her potty mouth would describe him.

"Do you think Glenn'll let me ride his surfer?" said Tank.

"Surfboard," I said. "He's the surfer, or wants people to think he is. No. He won't."

"I like Glenn, Glenn is nice," said Tank. I wondered if he liked Glenn because he was a little kid and couldn't distinguish between assholes and saints or was it because he was the type who was born to see only the good in everyone which is to say superficial and maybe naive. The idea that he was one of the latter brought back the chorus of "Dock of the Bay." I tried to focus instead on the Steve Cropper guitar part which was classic Stax/Volt gospel-inflected, thank-you-Jesus Truth, but the weary sentiment of the chorus rolled in like those never ending waves.

We crossed the highway and walked out on the beach. It was low tide and the sand was shell-less and hard packed. Near the water Glenn stripped off his shirt and sunglasses, handed them off to Angie, and strutted down to the ocean. I could feel Tank's excitement even though I was not looking at him. He perked up like a dog who smells a squirrel in the brush. Where was my own interest in the mess I'd left behind? My daddy had gone off for the worst time. A small chunk of my brother's ear was lying among his shorn locks on the porch boards. Stolen truck, stolen shirts. Surely Frosty had alerted the authorities, claiming I stole all that merchandise. I'd serve time for a bag of Ruffles not a single ridged chip of which I actually got to savor. They'd hang me with kidnapping too. All this to worry about and here I was following my sister down to watch her surfer-cool boyfriend paddle around in the total lack of surf.

Angie had stripped off her waitress uniform, laid it out on the sand, and was stretched out in a bikini, smoking and shading her eyes from the sun. Tank ran down to her and said, "Can I go get in the water?"

"Ask your daddy," she said.

"He ain't my daddy. My daddy is your daddy."

She rolled her eyes behind her sunglasses. I remembered her story about my mama's affair, how that was what was wrong with my daddy. I felt sorry for her, making up such a story when it was clear that it was something in his blood that made him act the way he did. I understood it though. Believing it meant she had the power to make a man lie out in the dirt yard howling for a way dead dog. Golf-club televisions.

"You can get in up to your knees, okay?" I told Tank. "But take your shirt and shorts off."

"Go in my underwear?"

"It's okay," I said. He stripped to his brand-new Fruit of the Looms and ran bowlegged down to the water.

I sat down in the sand next to Angie. She ignored me for her cigarette. Sometimes she shielded her eyes to watch Glenn, who had yet to catch a wave.

"What's he waiting for?"

"At least he's out there."

"I don't want to be out there."

"Yeah, well, I don't want you to be here. I'm fucking going to kill that Carla bitch."

"She didn't tell me," I said.

"God, you're such a hopeless liar."

"Don't you want to know what happened?"

"You're going to tell me anyway."

She smoked. She shielded her eyes. I watched my little brother Tank play in the surf. It was hard for me to believe the way my sister acted. She was so different from me. If I was mudcreek, she was chlorine. Knowing her made me feel at a very early age that I knew nothing about people. I have vowed many times not to speak to them or look them in the eye for surely when you do, it's all over, the trouble begins. At the same time the only means of death I truly fear in this world is loneliness. When my classmates on the bus back out to Moody Loop used to argue over what was worse, drowning, burning to death, suffocating, falling, etc., I never said how none of those things scared me so much as dying unloved or alone.

I looked at my sister and saw her years from now behind a cash register, her eyes flat, the fire having burned out from a constant and high temperature ire. She would talk nonstop to strangers and friends alike and their responses, if she even heard them, would never matter to her. We were as different as could be. I was actually a decent listener. It's just that I dreaded talking to people because so often they would turn out, like my sister, to be talking to themselves. I would sit there, like Otis, watching the tide roll in, wasting time.

"Well?" she said. "Where the hell is Carter?"

"He stayed with him."

"Why? He hates him. It's you two who think he hung the fucking moon. Carter's the only one of y'all with any damn sense."

She was right to think that Carter was more like her and less like me and Tank. But he did not hate my daddy. He loved my daddy. She loved him too. We all loved each other, even as scathed and unraveled as we were. If at any time we didn't, the hell with us all.

"He does not either hate him."

"Whatever," she said. "Just tell me what happened."

I told her. She kept stopping me though.

"Wait," she said, "What do you mean he stuffed bananas in his mouth?"

"He just crammed them in, stem, peel, and all."

"Fucking gorilla. Go on."

But she stopped me again.

"What do you mean his earlobe?"

I described what I saw.

"Why didn't you leave if you had the keys?"

"You know how he is. Sometimes it doesn't last long."

"You can't ever tell by looking at him how long it's going to last. Therefore you really fucked up."

"What happened to Termite?" I asked. I guess I wanted to take the pressure off. I didn't care to hear how I'd fucked up since she'd run off not long after my mama and we'd yet to hear word one from her and I knew she would do what she could for us but that she'd act like we were the biggest pains in the ass she'd ever known.

"Fucking Carla," she said. "What do you care what happened to him?"

"I guess I'm not the only one who fucks up."

"You have no idea what you're talking about. Termite or

anyone else I date is none of your goddamn business. That's number one. Number two, where is Carter now? Is he safe? What happened to him? How could you leave him?"

"How could you?"

"I don't recall anyone holding a pair of scissors to anybody's throat the day I bolted."

"All kind of bad things could have happened since you left."

"Could have or did?"

"All I'm saying is, how would you know? We never heard from you again. Her either. Seems like you can't go around acting like you give a damn if you run off and we never hear jack from you."

"Maybe I was about to call? Anyway I don't have to take this shit from you. You might share his name but you're not my daddy."

When she said that, it made me scared.

"I never thought he'd do a thing like that," I said.

"Me neither, " she said. "I never would of left y'all with him if I thought he'd take it out on anything but the television."

"She didn't know either."

"Of course she didn't."

"She needs to know."

"Needs to know what? You don't even know what happened after you left. You need to go back up there and get Carter."

"How come I have to do it? Why can't you?"

"Because I have a goddamn job and I didn't steal anybody's truck."

"Those sound like piss poor reasons to me," I said. But she
wasn't paying attention. All of a sudden she stood up.

"Hey," she said in a far less bitchy and more urgent tone.
"Where's Tank?"

I'd been drawing in the sand with my fingers the whole
time I'd been talking to her. Angie was on her feet and I followed. She ran to the water's edge and called to Glenn, who
was paddling around just past the breakers as if every wave
that passed were beneath his awesome level of skill. I thought
Tank had tried to swim out to him. But Tank could not swim.

Glenn was paddling around, Angie was screaming, and I
just stood there at the water's edge, the tide rolling in, the sun
on the water, my little brother's ear falling from the high
white clouds, Otis singing "Dock," a little voice seeping up
out of the water and then a hand, tiny and wet, grabbing my
own.

I looked down and saw Tank.

"Where the hell did you get to?"

"I went up there to pee," he said, pointing to the dunes.

Angie turned and looked down at him. For a second she
tried to look like her usual disconnected self. Then she
scooped him up in her skinny arms and hugged him so hard
he choked.

"Put me down, put me down," said Tank.

But she kept squeezing him. He must have felt her tears

because he melted into her bony-shouldered self. I saw what I needed to see. I reached out and rubbed Tank's head. There is a photograph of my mama holding Carter when he was about the age Tank was on the beach that afternoon. Carter had his head burrowed into my mother's shoulder though you could see his eyes peeking out at the photographer, just like Tank was peeking at me. He looked puzzled but not uncomfortable. Glenn came striding out of the water. He looked at the three of us, shrugged, and headed up the beach. "Stupid fucker," Angie said under her breath. Tank laughed. I thought, I'll just run and get Carter. We don't need any mama and daddy. We got the ocean, the pier.

But then I remembered why I came here.

"Where is she?" I asked.

"Who?" said Tank. "Who, who?"

"Goddamn all y'all," said Angie. She was more like me then than I ever would have thought, and I was going to get in there while the window was open.

"Where?"

"She don't want to see us," Angie said.

"Who?" said Tank.

"Tell me where."

"She's living in Bulkhead. Some place called the Promise Land."

"Who is? Who is living in that place?" said Tank.

"No *d* on Promise," said Angie. She looked at me and laughed. "No fucking *d*."

"I'll be back," I said.

"Where you going?" said Tank.

"To the truck to get something."

"Hurry the fuck up," said Angie. "I've got shit to do today."

I said, "I'll be back."

"Joel Junior, Joel Junior," said Tank as I started up to the beach road.

"Ssssh," I heard Angie said. "Don't call him that."

"What do I supposed to call him?" asked Tank.

"Call him Mario," she said. "That's what his shirt says."

"Hey Mario," Tank called.

"Hey Ed," I said to Tank.

"Bye Mario," Tank said.

"Bye Ed," I told Tank.

FIVE

M Y MAMA LOVED ARETHA. She had all her records. They were the only ones she owned. Like a lot of girls, she would listen to whatever you happened to be playing, but she wasn't big on spending her money on records like my daddy was. He had his albums lined up along one wall of the living room in alphabetical order. They stretched the length of the room. Me and Tank and Carter would spend hours looking at the covers, reading the liner notes, imagining ourselves somewhere in the montage on the front of *Sgt. Pepper's* or, I'm speaking for myself here, in the arms of that naked black woman on the cover of Santana's *Abraxas*. Since my daddy was out of work a lot and unable to do much past assist people when he was gainfully employed, we could have used that record money for other things surely. Shoes. Potatoes. I believe my mama let him spend all the money he wanted on his music because it gave him such pleasure. Also it pacified us boys who could make some noise at times, not to mention trash some square footage, accidentally knock stuff over, etc.

Most of the time my mama let my daddy play DJ and if she did not like something—which, she had her dislikes, for instance, Laura Nyro who reminded her of her least favorite and extremely whiny sister—she just did not listen to it. The exception was when she was cooking. Then it was her turn to choose the music. She nearly always chose Aretha.

The Queen of Soul. Everyone in our house worshipped Aretha. A hush would come over the house when my mother would play *Lady Soul.* Her voice blew through the rooms like the first stirrings of an approaching storm. Curtains lifted, blinds chattered, dogs lifted their muddy ears from the cool-down holes they dug beneath bushes. In the kitchen, onions sizzled in percussive accompaniment to that blue gospel Muscle Shoals sound. When she hit those highest notes it felt like the whole house was rising up off its foundations, about to float off to some place where lovers came back to you and men did right by their women and everybody, whether they believed in Jesus or not, said—each morning they woke up, before they even put on their makeup—a little prayer for you.

The songs my mama loved best were the ones written by Aretha's sister Carolyn, especially "Ain't No Way." I cannot listen to "Ain't No Way" without thinking that Aretha's sister Carolyn had my mama and daddy in mind when she was writing it. The woman in that song is trying to love her man but something in him (or *not* in him) just won't let her. It made me think my mama loved my daddy but loving him the way he was just tired her out so much she had to get away and rest from it all. How could she take us with her and ever get the rest she needed?

I had "Ain't No Way" in my head as I left Tank on the beach with Angie. I was giving my mama the benefit of the doubt even though it turned out she was in Bulkhead which was only an hour or so north of Bottomsail. We might have even gone to Bulkhead fishing with my daddy and run into her at the Sanitary which she loved their hush puppies. If I could keep "Ain't No Way" in my head I could not fault her for leaving us. My mama was devoted to my daddy though she wasn't anybody's fool. She just could not help him when he was off. About all she could do was load us in the pickup and haul us over to her parents. My grandmother smelled like a pickle. I missed Tank already so I sang out loud some Aretha to drown out my desire to turn around and go fetch him and take him with me to see our mama. This got me up to the pier where the pickup sat alone in the parking lot, the pier fisherman having cleared out during daylight. I did not want to be seen around my daddy's vehicle but I needed a clean shirt out of there and also I thought if I left the keys in it, someone would surely steal it and I therefore could not be hauled up for theft of a car that someone else had stolen. It occurred to me that Frosty might not have turned me in after all, given his feelings toward my daddy. What it was, when he was assisting a roofer, my daddy had done some work on Frosty's house and then because he was out of work he had patched a hole in the store for no money. Of course Frosty extended credit to our family and my father hated dearly the idea that he had to buy on credit but he knew he could not work steady and that my mother's wages would not support the six of us without some credit. That's about the only way Frosty would find you likable, if you give him something for nothing.

I fetched the shirt from the floorboard, the bag with the peanut butter and the loaf of Merita, some tapes of my daddy's including the Persuasions, the Barkays, Joe Tex, Rufus and Carla and Marvin Gaye and Tammi Terrell, and stuck the key in the ignition. I rolled down the windows to make it easier for the no-good thieving bastard who happened to stroll by and see the dangling keys. On the one hand there was a good chance I could have made it to Bulkhead as the truck would have already been discovered if Frosty had called the cops, but on the other there I was fourteen years old and driving around like I had my license. I had everything in the grocery bag old Frosty made such a production of flapping open for me. I tucked in my work shirt to make it appear that I had just gotten off work.

Everybody that passed me was just riding around, driving with their hands out the window and in slow motion beach time, so I walked a good two miles in the boiling sun, exhausted, missing Tank. Now it was two little brothers I had left behind. I would come back for them both, I told myself. First Carter, then Tank. I wasn't so worried about Tank with

Angie, for I'd seen what I needed to see to know she'd take good care of him. Anyway I'd be back in a couple of days. It just got to be too much, carting Tank around, having to ask him did he need to go to the bathroom all the time, listening to that strange little alien off-kilter hum he kept up when he was playing, dealing with his million questions, why do they call it a sound, who lives at Bulkhead, who, why, where? It got to where I was smacking him liberally. That boy did not need smacking, he needed holding. Angie would bygod have to step up to the plate.

Walking over the humped drawbridge, watching the sun glint off the yachts in the distance, I wondered why there was no *d* in Promise Land. Angie thought this was funny but to me it was a real bad sign. As if there were nothing promised but the people who lived there were filled with unfulfilled or empty promises, about which I knew a little something.

At the highest hump of the bridge, I looked back over my shoulder at the ocean. The girls in the family fled to the beach, but where would I go if I could go? Well, no matter how I looked at it I was still fourteen years old which this limited my options considerably despite the amount of junk I'd had to take on prematurely. My daddy going off, then my mama leaving, then my sister. And now me, leaving Carter on the porch screaming not because of his earlobe which, what could he do about that, wasn't as if they were going to sew it back on, it was the loss of his long blond curls upsetting him. Now me, leaving him and Tank too behind. I figured a city would be better than any beach. In a city they say nobody gets up in your business. A fourteen-year-old boy would attract no more notice than an alley cat or a no-name dog in a city as opposed to Bulkhead, which was small enough so that I'd stick out on those three or four streets.

I reached the beach highway and stuck out my thumb. I had never hitched before, having nowhere to hitch to, plus I always had my little tagass brothers along, our beat up bikes to ride, but I knew enough to know that you stood less of a chance catching a ride if you were carrying a paper bag which made you look homeless or escaped-prisoner. I made two sandwiches, stood on the shoulder gumming peanut butter, wrapped a spare shirt around my waist and ditched the bag. He left with only the clothes on his back, I said about myself. This made me laugh, which was not at all a good thing, yukking it up to yourself with your thumb stuck out, who would pick up such a maniac, ain't no way. Wipe that grin off your face, I said aloud, and this too made me laugh. It was hopeless. I'd have to walk the forty-seven miles to Bulkhead if I did not get ahold of myself. It was that dying time of day downeast when the big sky and flat fields turned golden and a haze rose from the fields and the pines turned from sharply needled and ominous to a muted blue-green smear. Marshland on either side of the road, tall grass swaying in the truck gusts. A crooked-legged crane stood in a channel ignoring the beach traffic which within seconds turned from individual cars and trucks to a stream of illumination. My chances of catching a ride were growing slimmer by the second. Still I had to force myself to take my situation seriously, to tune out the Aretha soaring somewhere in the background, which I tried but quickly failed to do.

A ratty Datsun pulled over five minutes later. A Mexican with a kindly smile. He smelled of gas and his hat and jeans were black with grease but when I told him I was going to Bulkhead he nodded wildly and said, "Bulkhead, sí, yo tambien," and I relaxed into the sprung bucket seat. He only knew enough English to let me know we would not be trading life stories which was fine by me. We listened to mariachi music which may have been the first time I'd heard it except for snatches in the fields when me, Tank, and Carter would ride up to town on our bikes. It put me in the mind of a carnival. The accordion made me miss Tank, who would have hummed crazily along with the song had he been in that car. He would have poked his head between the bucket seats and asked, What's he singing about, what's the name of that record, how old are you, what's your name? Tank and his crazy-ass questions. The accordion and the syncopated standup bass and the plaintive two-part harmonies washed over me like waves of salt water. Music was to blame for taking me places so far back in time. If there was no music I would not have a thing to do with my daddy. He would be a pitiful figure thrashing like a banked salamander in the gravel drive. Without Aretha my mother would not exist either. A selfish run-off-because-she-could-not-take-it bitch. Carter in the yard wrapped head to toe in a garden hose screaming the words to "Susie-Q." Tank begging peanut butter and raisins upon celery—ants on a log—and some dang

Curtis. Never mind we're out of celery and the raisins are hard as pebbles, just play that boy some Curtis and he's pig blissful. Let's say we'd grown up like so many in a house where instead of music there was a television. I just don't see how you're supposed to survive on the fumes of, say, *Gilligan's Island*.

Que bonito es querer, sang the Mariachitos.

What's he saying what's he saying? said Tank from the backseat.

Love is wonderful, said the Mexican. Wide and kind was his smile.

About once a week my daddy took us to Dusselbach's which sold couches, tables, chairs, record players, records. We wandered about the showroom while he stood studiously in front of the rows of albums, flipping them back and forth in their bins. Way in the back of the store, lounging on the wings of a sectional sofa, we heard the slap of the covers. He was looking for that song which would lift him soaring above the access road of his life, the assisting of pipe fitters and church steeple builders, the changing of diapers, the trying so hard not to go damn *off*. Maybe sometimes his song drowned out those voices in his head. Slip away, sang Clarence Carter instead of some combination of God on High (which I'm not even sure when he was *on* my daddy even believed in) and, say, Neil Armstrong, moonwalker, telling him to to go outside and call the neighbor's dead dog back from the dark grave wherein he lay. I don't know what qualifies me to go around saying what goes on in anybody's head, especially my daddy's which as heads go is a complicated one with a lot of static and buzz and humming and interference from other planets and to hear him talk occasional contact from the Parliament/Funkadelic mothership. On the other hand, who is better qualified than me? My mama who ran away to of all places bygod Bulkhead?

What's the name of that song? said Tank.

Declarate inocente, said the Mexican.

Plead innocent, I said before Tank could ask him to translate.

Armed with his records my daddy would come collect us from the mock bedrooms of the nether corners of Dusselbach's.

I like that song right there, said Tank to the Mexican, his new best friend.

Daddy, daddy, what'd you get? He'd show us his purchase: an Al Green album upon which the Reverend covered Hank Williams ("I'm So Lonesome I Could Cry," one of my daddy's all time favorites) and the Bee Gees ("How Can You Mend a Broken Heart"). We all three knew the story about Al Green's girlfriend dumping a pot of boiling grits in his lap. We knew he survived and found Jesus in his heart. We knew about Sam Cooke getting shot in a motel by the woman worked behind the counter who he thought was hiding some girl he wanted to get with who had run off from his room when he'd tried to pull her dress off, taking his pants with her. My daddy didn't spare any details. We knew that Marvin Gaye had been shot by his very own daddy, and that he, like our own daddy, was prone to going off. (That one got away with me the worst, a gone-off genius getting shot by someone who like as not took care of him and protected him and loved him when nobody else would. It got away with me so bad I almost could not listen to Marvin though when he was singing with Tammi Terrell he seemed so young and innocent and committed to love instead of on his later stuff when he got all political, not that there's anything wrong with that, but those duets with Tammi did not bring me down like, say, "Mercy Mercy Me" or "What's Going On" could, knowing how he met his end.) We all knew about Otis because my daddy dove to the bottom of that Wisconsin lake and held Otis's head up off his chest while his last song ticked out of him and green water filled his lungs. We knew just what the price was for singing your ass off night after night. My daddy didn't even really need to share these horrible facts for me to understand. I heard it in their very voices as they spilled out of our boxy console stereo, drifted from the busted and staticky speakers of the pickup. Heartache, shame, regret, devil telling you turn this way, whiskey, everybody's woman but your own, poverty, betrayal, belt-wielding, scripture-quoting daddys, people telling you over and over how you're nothing but sorry, or maybe even worse, telling you you're the greatest thing who ever walked, I heard all that and I knew where it would take you. I knew that their pain was somehow setting me free. I knew their hard lives were allowing me to live with my daddy and not blame my run-off mama and even better than just living with them it was letting me love them in all their sorriness, waste, and neglect.

Then we would get in the pickup and on the way home my daddy would let us rip the plastic off the albums and look at the covers. All three of us boys riding up front, Tank in the middle. We would unfold the album and read aloud all the song titles, who wrote them, even how long they were. We would memorize the order. We would look at who played what instrument on which track. (We knew, for instance, every Stones song featuring Billy Preston, had got to where we could pick out his swirling organ up under the noise of a train-coming-down-the-track tornado.)

How about that one, that one's right pretty too, said Tank.

La llorna loca, said our driver.

Crazy woman, I whispered to Tank.

At home we would be out of the house even before the pickup cranked off or rocked to a stop. We would crowd up under the speakers of the stereo waiting on our daddy who was the first always to drop the needle on the virgin vinyl. He'd fuss with the stylus first, blowing away the dust, his breath amplified by the speakers, a sibilant boom. We'd smell the plastic as the album heated up. By the time we'd played the album all afternoon (which we always did even if it didn't send us immediately, we'd play it till we knew every guitar and organ solo, every bass line, every word. The words we could not make out didn't bother us because we just made up our own) it would smell like it was about to melt.

Como un amanecer! announced the Mexican to Tank without having been asked.

Like a new day! I said, nodding.

But Tank was not there and I do not know Spanish.

We rolled off the highway into Bulkhead. It was not a new day, it was the same old one in which I left Tank with my foul-mouthed sister without saying good-bye, the day after the one in which I left Carter on the porch with my scissors-wielding daddy. All of a sudden it hit me what I'd gotten real good at: love.

"Donde somethinganother," said the Mexican. We'd pulled off into the parking lot of an auto parts store. Bulkhead was a strip of chicken-and-biscuit joints, car dealerships, pawn-shops, bars, chain stores. I spied a Dollar Store. I smiled weakly at the driver, having grown tired of the mariachi music. He pointed up the road. His smile too had grown tepid and worried around the edges.

Oh, okay, right, he wanted me to get out.

I watched the Datsun pull away. Adios! Almost immediately I missed the mariachi music. The carnies had struck their tents and their rusty rides and taken off in the middle of the night leaving only a trampled and trash-strewn field at the edge of town. To think our town could play host to such sparkling magic only to wake of a Sunday to find we'd dreamed it all from the dirt up. The sight of the muddy field shamed us until the weeds overtook it, and, later, mercifully, Clinton Herring's daddy who owned it planted some fast-spreading soybeans. Music fades and you're left with noth-ing. A brogan trampled field. Locks of blond hair carpeting porch boards. A string of lights that switches suddenly to a line of cars bearing strangers who would not stop for a boy in a floppy work shirt, singing to himself in Spanglish.

She would live by some water, my mama. If not the ocean, the sound or a creek. The Promise Land would promise at least a sliver of inlet. I walked the strip, followed the parade of cruising cars until I saw a sign for the so-called business district. They must have had sense enough to build a town on some water.

I entered a neighborhood of big old houses cut up into apartments. The yards were filled with cars. Aretha sang about a rose in Spanish Harlem. The porches were filled with families or drinkers, sometimes both. The rush of cars and other night noises turned magically into a tight Muscle Shoals rhythm section backing up Aretha, the smell of exhaust and garbage and spilled beer and something slightly sulfurous which I took to be whatever body of water my mama was living on. Aretha singing "You Send Me." Darling you do, you do, do. She sent me on down to street toward the Promise Land to find my mama. Babies say mama. No *d*. I was hungry again. Also bone tired. My feet swole up in my Adidas. I'm sorry Carter. I loved you but I favored Tank. If Tank was the favored why did I leave him with Angie? Let's say that like she claimed she had none of my daddy in her. That left only my mama's blood in her veins, my mama who had run off and left her boys in the hands of a man prone to flat-out neglect. That meant Angie herself was going to run off. She'd leave Tank with some giant of a man name of Termite. Or to fend for himself in a house trailer with beach roaches I knew to be the size of blue crabs. Tank would be one of those kids you read about discovered by a neighbor fending for themselves after having been abandoned by all those put on this earth to tend to his welfare. That would be me. What had I done? Ain't no way that was going to happen because if I went around assuming the apple don't fall far from the tree in the case of my sister, foul-mouthed inheritor of my mama's tendency to run off, what then did that say about my own future?

The idea of having to plan my baby steps within my daddy's limits sent me staggering. Ants in my head tunneling their bad bad thoughts through the sand, visible to passersby and porch sitters as my flesh was transparent, they could see my brain. You try to hide something and the more you try to hide the more everyone notices. I staggered down that street like a blind man. Aretha sang "Amazing Grace." She sang the ever-loving hell out of a wretch like me. The apartments fell away to a block of low storefronts. From one I heard the dim rumble of drum and bass and then a tinny organ rising out of the beat. A large woman, black and sharply dressed, sidestepped up onto the curb from a high-idling Buick.

"Can you show me the way to the Promise Land?" I cried out.

"Lord God, child, come right along here," she said. She took my hand and I followed. Was she not the same woman back home in Trent who had tried to help Tank when I pushed his obstinate ass out of the pickup at the laundry so I could steal the very shirt I wore on my back? She showed up places to save us. Whenever we most needed her. If people love you and you're in trouble that trouble rumbles in their stomach. She had changed her church hat and she had maybe put on a few pounds but she was still wearing those shiny high heels. Plus she knew where the Promise Land was.

"I'm trying to find my mama."

"You getting ready to meet your Heavenly Father," she said.

We got closer to the music. She pushed open the door to a storefront with blacked-out plate-glass windows and we were right up inside it, that music.

Or else the music was inside of us. If you were lucky enough to hear it it never left you, which was why those people without it (like my sister, who could give a spit what was on the radio and never seemed to care about my daddy's records which was why she had to leave, why she was maybe on the money when she suggested she was not really our sister) couldn't just up and let it in their hearts. Aretha strayed, according to my daddy she had some hard times, but she never really left the church. She was at heart always a gospel singer. About Jesus I don't think so but how could you not know how deeply my daddy's music sprung right up out of the church? You could hear it in those high notes Aretha nailed, a rapturous spirit pouring out of her. It would touch you, too, if you let it. You didn't need to be, like Aretha, a preacher's daughter. You didn't even need to go to church.

There were only six or seven people in the pews, more than that up on the crude plywood stage. A preacher sweated in the corner. Every one of them looked long at me when we entered the room. A dirty stringy white boy holding hands with their Miss Whoever she was, I never did catch her name. Well, he look like he in need of some salvation, that's for sure. Ain't no way he don't need God's love. The band was just bubbling, all instrumental, I could feel a chorus coming on, but they were waiting on the water to boil, which directly right after we sat and my tired-ass toes started to tap, the water surely did. The chorus broke, the two women singers beat the ever-loving hell out of their tambourines and broke right up into something high and soaring, a single phrase sung over and over until it made, each time, more and more and finally the most ever sense: light in this world, light in this world, light in this world.

Everyone knew the words and lifted their voices up to the dropped ceiling of the storefront.

God in Heaven I felt lifted myself. The ants went away, I was a handsome sapsucker not wearing a work shirt bearing the name of Mario which I outright stole, my little brothers were fine, my mama was back home in the kitchen cooking and listening to Aretha build with her very breath a bridge over some deeply troubled water, girls wanted me, no pimples, nobody pointing to my exposed shins in the hallway of the high school and hollering, Where the flood at? And the only *off* my daddy was? Off to work of a morning.

For some the world they walk through is more than

enough. They know to make their way through it, know exactly *how* to. For me it was always like that showroom in the back of Dusselbach's: someone else's furniture, phony living rooms, stiff and new-smelling, uncomfortable and unfamiliar. If I inherited anything at all from my daddy it was a desire for music to make me to feel at home in this world. Sam and Otis and Curtis and Sly, Rufus and Carla and Aretha and Isaac, the brothers Isley and the siblings Staples — they let me in my own house. See, I'd get locked out a lot. And I'd have to call them up and listen to them unlock the door and let me back in.

When the singing stopped, the ants came tunneling back. I felt real white. Some small children who had come during the singing were staring at me in a way only small children can stare. Tank, please forgive me. Did she even have enough sense to make his ass go to bed at a decent time? If not she'd pay for it tomorrow as he would be crosser than hell. I had a sudden flash of the living room where my sister and her surfer boyfriend were hanging out. A low, sprung-seat couch upon which sat Angie, surfer Glenn, and a whole other couple. Tank sprawled out beneath them on the beer-stained carpet. The television was on but the sound was turned down. Back and forth goes the bong. Someone, Glenn I guess, has given him a Game Boy to play with. He's thumbing that cheap piece of green plastic and my sister is playing the bygod radio, not even the oldies station which even Tank knows is the only station worth listening to. Some station called Beach 95 which is mostly ads for car dealerships and tanning booths and occasionally some Top 40 trash of the most useless sort.

I felt my lifted spirit plummet, thinking of Tank and that cheesy music and him the only one in the room half-listening to it as the others were too caught up in their stoner dialogue which in my sister's case consisted largely of upper-case obscenities. Carter, you only went along to get along. I could tell you were faking it. You would sing with us but the words were only coming out of your mouth, not your very being. Carter, I'm sorry, it's no reason not to love somebody. It's just, why did you have to climb out of that truck?

"It's not my fault," I said aloud in the quiet of the church, in the middle of the fiery preaching. I was hardly aware of the preacher up there in front of me, stomping around, quoting scripture, looking stern like we're all of us about to die.

"Hush now," said my savior.

The children snickered.

"I have to go," I said, and before she could answer I was up and out of that room.

Well, the music had stopped. I owed nobody nothing when it ceased. Just got to get on down the road to a place where I can receive the signal full on.

Outside I kept looking over my shoulder to see did she send one of those children to bring me back in but she must have thought there is some that don't even know how to take His love in they hearts. Or else she was glad to be shy of me. I thought she'd maybe turn up again before it was all over. Or maybe she'd storm in that trailer where my sister and her surfer friends were goofing on some TV with the sound turned down. Dude, you would not fucking believe what happened last night at the crib, they'd say to everyone who wandered in their surf shop the next day. I could see Tank look up from his Game Boy. His face when he got startled was so pure and baby-looking. Frozen, innocent, it was the only time he was ever really still. The church lady pulls her girth up the stairs and pushes in the trailer. My sister's friends cower as she plants herself in the doorway. Give me that Game Boy, she says to Tank. Or maybe it's give me that play toy, I don't know, all I know is she slips the thing into her pocketbook which swings threateningly from her arm, takes Tank by the hand and thunders into the night, bringing my little brother back to me.

Out on the street the other storefronts were shut tight. Only light in this world was the streetlight and the lights of cars passing steady as a river inches away from me. The street was one-way which struck me as exactly right. I only needed one choice. I felt lost and lonely and all I wanted was a bath and to find my mother. How could I fall so swiftly from that rapturous height? I imagined wandering the rest of my life in search of a stronger signal, a place where the music reached me without static or disturbance. I was not like him, not at all, it was voices he heard, not Aretha, Arthur Conley, Deena Parker. Music for him was a drowning-out of those voices telling him to stuff bananas in the mouth of his middle son. Therefore we were exact opposites. There was one spot in the room I shared with my little brothers where at night when we were supposed to be sleeping we could pick up WLS out of Chicago, 890 on the AM dial. It was over by the dresser drawers, a dip in the floorboards where moonlight fell on a no-cloud night. I'd put a little bit of masking tape there for my bare feet to feel. I would wait for them to fall asleep and then I'd shake their sideways-sleeping asses off me and wiggle out to that sweet spot, switch on the transistor my daddy bought me when I wasn't but Tank's age, listen to the Classic Soul hour, midnight to one in the morning, the signal traveling all the way down through Ohio across the river into Kentucky, bumping over the hills and hollers of West Virginia, shooting straight down the Valley of Virginia (I looked it up on one of my daddy's maps) to cross the red-clay piedmont and reach me up home, just a spit from the sea. Just as people who love you feel your trouble rumbling in their stomachs, a song broadcast hundreds of miles away will be summoned by your need to hear it. I myself was not a boy in clothes about ready for the rag bag, half of them purloined, but radio waves coming through the swamps and pocosins, summoned down to Bulkhead by a mother's undying love for her oldest boy.

Have you seen the Promise Land? I asked a boy who looked to be lingering at the ass end of teenaged, as if he hadn't quite got it together to pass over into his twenties. His sideburns were bristly and sharply razored to hide his extended chin, which all they did was exclamation point to it if you ask me. A tight T-shirt when he ought to of gone relaxed fit. The reason I asked him was, he was the only one to ask.

"You know, I just *did* see it," he said, proof that I asked the right question at the right time. Proof of my mama, drawing me closer. Look: Frosty, Carla, magic caster, Angie, the kindly Mexican, the church lady, all of them when you think about it form a line orchestrated by my mama's desire to see me again. Even my daddy going off could be considered in this light. What it was, she'd hung out her wash between that high-rise hotel and another building and it was fixing to pour and she was reeling in her line. I was being passed from person to person on my way back into her wide-open window.

"You wanting to see it?" he said.

Sometimes I want to be Tank. Spread-eagle facedown on a pier mumbling to crustaceans about Otis. People stepping right over me as if nothing's wrong with this picture. Tank don't have to act right. He's got me to look out for him, asking him does he got to go, stealing shirts, buying him Swee-TARTS so he can walk around humming off-key and asking crazy questions and deciding he likes people randomly like surfer Glenn who he ought not to like and the kindly Mexican which he got that one right. He was half-right. But not all there. They say that about my daddy but Tank is not supposed to be all there. All of him has not even supposed to have arrived yet. That's why I wouldn't mind being Tank sometimes. I can claim that part of me gives a damn is in the mail.

"Yeah, I do," I said. "I want to see the Promise Land. "

"Well I will take you straight to it," he said, "but first I got to ask you a favor."

"Okay, ask."

"Well, I got to show you."

"Show me a favor?"

I didn't have time for his mess. I could smell the beer on him when I got up close and the longer I talked to him the drunker he looked.

"Naw, man, un-unnh. You got it all wrong."

"Okay," I said, as if this made some sense. It dawned on me he wasn't allowed back in that pool room. I thought of going in there myself for it seemed like someone in there would know the whereabouts of the Promise Land.

"Follow me," he said. He took off down a alley.

"Hey, wait," I said.

"I thought you were wanting the Promise Land."

"I am."

"Well, it ain't gonna come to you."

"It's down there?"

"I told you I got to *something* a favor." The word he used where I have substituted "something" was swallowed, or something else stomach- or throat-wise was going on and I didn't care to ask him please repeat that. He had stopped and was looking at my shirt. "Mario, I'm Landers," he said. He looked at you after everything he said in a lingering way as if expecting some sort of reaction. But there wasn't anything to react to. I have seen this type tic before but only in people who say shit you don't know what to say back to them about.

Then he took off again, thank goodness. We came out on another street. It was one way going the opposite from the one we'd been on. Away from the water. Away from the Promise Land. Away from my mama.

I stopped at the sight of it.

"What's the matter?" said Landers. "Come on, it's just a little ways."

I felt so anxious I could not move. I felt like every small thing I ever had was lost to me. All because I had detoured slightly down a alley following drunk-wanting-a-reaction Landers, thinking I was for just a little while Tank.

Landers pointed to a car. Rather, it was one of those half-car/half-trucks. I don't care for hybrids. Broccoliflower, Ray Charles's country album. My daddy didn't care for that album and neither did I. The half-car/half-truck put me in rueful mind of *Modern Sounds in Country Western Music*, Vols. 1 and 2 by Ray Charles. I know it's not the same thing, Ray Charles and what they call a crossover, but to me it's similar. It's hard enough to be one thing, be it truck or big brother or landmark soul stirrer.

"I got to show you something," said Landers.

I had to stop thinking I wanted to be Tank because I was too old to be acting like Tank. Okay, what you got to show me? Tank would say. But I was too old. I had got sidetracked and was going upriver, away from the signal, opposite direction of that sweet music. I have been old for so many days. Which is why mostly I just want to go live on a hill near a silo. My kitchen will be in a basement. The house will slant down the hill so that the ass end will be level with the planet earth. The head of the basement will be up under ground. In the heat of the summer I will take all my meals in the kitchen plus sleep, do puzzles, and listen to music up in there. A car ought to be a car, truck all truck. Once when he was three Tank asked me did houses live inside or outside. His question got away with me big-time, liked to made me cry, I don't know why, I guess because I could not answer it and also it stirred up something so deep inside me only music could normally reach it. The walls of my basement kitchen will be of an ancient, dusty brick and quite thick. Rugs on the floor would be nice in the winter. Landers was walking right out into traffic. I was watching from the safety of the sidewalk. The Queen of Soul was singing "Call Me." My mother stood at the sink running water into a teakettle. I don't trust any hybrid. You either live inside or outside, either you hear the song or you got no ear. The thick and ancient dusty brick will retain heat in the winter and keep me cool in the heat of the summer. The water bubbled over as my mother stared out the window. Call me the minute you get there, my mother sang along with Aretha. In the summer I would pull up the rugs so my toes could feel the earth up under the brick floor. Cars were swerving around Landers who had kneeled down and was fiddling with something up under the dashboard. It's either a car or a truck it seems to me. The water bubbled out of the teapot and on down the drain. "Come here, come here," said Landers. He was waving me out into the road and cars were providing a horn section to the song in my head and in my mother's which was "Call Me." I got to show you something, sang Aretha. I stepped out into the road. Landers

waving me over to where he crouched holding a tube con-
nected to the dash. That half-car/half-truck was all over ugly.
"Blow on this," said Landers. "Do what?" I said. "Just blow on
it, I want to show you something." "Show me what?" "Goddamn, country, just blow on the motherfucker if you want to
see the Promise Land." I took it in my hand and looked at it.
"It won't fucking bite just blow like you would a whistle."
Cool in the heat of summer, toasty in the dead of winter.
Call me, my mother sang with Aretha as I blew into the tube
and Landers said, "Or like you would your boyfriend, you little redneck," and pushed me away nearly into a pickup
which though it damn near ran over me was all-the-way
pickup, not half Chevrolet or something, I couldn't tell what
half the car was because Landers had that ugly specimen
cranked and had pulled out into traffic before I could even
move out of the middle of the river of cars going the wrong
way from babies say mama I hate a hybrid call me call me I
don't care what time it is day or night just call me the moment you get there.

SIX

MY LITTLE BROTHER Carter's favorite song was "Tighten Up," by Archie Bell and the Drells. He had it all memorized. Me and Tank had to perform this routine he'd worked out on the porch or in our room or wherever to "Tighten Up." He always got to be Archie Bell. Me and Tank were the Drells.

"What's a Drell anyway?" Tank was always wanting to know.

"I'll tell you one thing, Tank," I was always happy to tell him, "a Drell don't get paid as much as a Archie Bell."

We Drells doubled up as musicians and roadies. Archie Bell fined us if we took too long to tune his guitar or came in a half second late on the bridge. My daddy told us James Brown did this to his band too. The Hardest Working Man in Show Business sounded to me like the meanest boss in it too.

Archie Bell would holler at me. I'd throw down some rolling chords.

"Tighten up on that bass," Archie Bell would point at Tank. Tank would thump-pluck his air bass. It was twice the size of him. He could barely hold it if a wind was to blow across the porch.

There was the sweetest horn break in "Tighten Up." The thing about it is, I never would of tolerated being a Drell if I did not dearly love "Tighten Up." You could not listen to it and sit still. If you could you were either a dried-up school-teacher, a man like fat Frosty, too big to shake it, or perhaps I don't know a eunuch.

I went down to Bulkhead trying to find the Promise Land. Old Landers had me blow the breath of life into his butt-ugly hybrid. That half-bull/half-man we studied in Myths and Legends was another ugly sapsucker. I don't know why I prefer things all one way or all the other but it aggravates me no end to see something stuck in between. All this time Tank had been waiting on me to tell him did houses live inside or outside. Since Landers and his hybrid, Tank's question had come back to buzz me like a mosquito in the night. Bulkhead aggravated the question. Which is it, Joel Junior, said the still nighttime streets and open-mouthed alleys of what they wanted to call downtown Bulkhead. Inside or outside? It was like we won't even talking houses anymore. Can a boy be big damn brother and steal named shirts and negotiate with Frosty for a half tank of gas and some Ruffles and also answer to the song up inside his head? Or does he got to choose between the two to make his way through this world?

Carter lost his earlobe and worse than that to him I bet, his hair. Therefore, wandering around Bulkhead, I put "Tighten Up" on the box in his honor even if, as Archie Bell, he was all the time telling somebody what to do.

There are people in this world you just want to help but something in them won't let you. I believe Carter was like this. I wanted to be his brother and to love him like I did Tank, my daddy, my foul-mouthed sister, my mama, but Carter did not listen when I said stay in this boiling truck.

I loved Tank so I had to leave him behind. If you love someone, set them free. What does that mean? It's not for me to question, I'm just one of the Drells, it's not like I'm Archie Bygod Big-Time King-Bee Bell.

Bulkhead, Bulkhead: why'd you get so all of a sudden quiet? I walked up the one-way street going the wrong way. Kids my age and older cruising in their jacked-up, fat-tired vehicles called me names. You want to help people but they won't let you. "Tighten up on that guitar," I yelled at one of them, which this cracked my tired ass up big-time.

Oh I was so old. I just wanted to reach whatever body of water dead-ended this miserable town. Nothing's promised you in the Promise Land. It's just a low-lying area where people'll tell you low lies.

I came to a strip of grass resembling a park and there, rolling black with strips of white breaker, lay the sound. I stood on the bulkhead, staring out at the water, wondering couldn't they think up a better name for this place? Why not, say, Sidewalk?

Did my mama come here because she craved the Sanitary

hush puppies. That sounds like a question but I'm going to go ahead and leave off the mark because I don't want to know the answer. Something probably like: here is where my crazy-ass husband and aggravating boys particularly are *not*.

She didn't want to see us, said my sister. I remembered that and it liked to make me cry. What kept me from breaking down was old Archie Bell barking at me to tighten up.

A bench appeared to which I availed myself. It was way dark. But you could see the surf and the lights of the tankers headed up to the port and you could see across the water tiny beach towns twinkling. Maybe my mama had gone over to one of those places for the evening. Maybe she had located some tastier hush puppies. It pained me to think that tastier hush puppies were all she had on her mind. So I conjured up those "Tighten Up" sessions on the porch. We'd put the speakers in the window, sling open the screens so nothing would be in the way of that sweet horn break. Carter would choreograph the bridge, me and Tank sidestep swaying while I pantomined trombone and Tank, sax. Carter, I meant to say Archie Bell (he'd get mad at us if we just called him Archie), would be hollering phrases he was wanting us to respond to: Hole up, he'd say and we'd repeat it. Check that out, *check that out*, What'd I say? *What'd he say?* I talked back to Carter for a while which put out of my head the idea that my mama had nothing in hers but the satisfying of some taste buds.

I thought someone else would happen by, that my mama would send them like she'd done kindly Mexican and the others. Even Landers. He allowed me to realize my potential and breathe to life a half-car/half-truck. This was something I previously had no iota I could pull off. He too was sent to me by my mama, his ugly attitude after I cranked his car for him all a part of tightening me up. It's a sad fact that people you try to help will do you like dirt.

I stretched out on the bench, on the bulkhead, waiting. Cars beeped the horn break of "Tighten Up." Though I am a fool for "Tighten Up" and it never fails to move me from the waist down, heading north from my belt buckle we are talking no whatsoever reaction. Ain't nothing wrong with a hip shaker. Repeated listenings still bring on the sway. But Tank favored "Dock of the Bay" which even if you took away those deeply sad lyrics — for surely the saddest notion of all is that nothing is going to change, everything will stay the same — would still strike you somewhere between the nervous stomach and the I-can't-take-it-no-more heart. Yet it moved your ass too. It was half-car/half-truck, much as I hated to call anything I favored after that blow-on-a-tube-to-crank-it crate.

It was interesting also that Carter favored "Tighten Up." The lyrics don't really stick in your head. Carter is a man of action. Witness his escape from the boiling truck. I wasn't going to go ahead and go on record as saying this was what led to the loss of his earlobe. All I'm saying is unlike Tank I think Carter was sometimes impatient with that movie one can conjure on the windshield of a boiling truck, the one with fair maidens laced up at the chest like Chuck Taylor tenny pumps and the grandpa from *Beverly Hillbillies* chasing Lady

Godiva. See, he just got bored. Whereas me and Tank could contentedly sit and wait for whoever it is destined to save us to bring their lateasses on.

Tank and me, we don't get bored. Carter and Angie, they get bored. Where did their boredom derive from? Some might argue from my mama, that it was her boredom that led her to leave four kids alone and unattended with a husband who had a whole drawer full of hospital discharge papers stashed away somewhere. (That was not even counting the withdrew-against-doctor's-advice papers which I assume he balled up in the parking lot of whatever institution he had bolted from.) But I knew she was fixing to send someone by there to pick me up, bring me to her, and it would not do, my thinking bad thoughts about her right before our reunion. Accusing someone of easy boredom, that's the same as saying they have nothing inside their head but pine straw. Why would I want to make that claim about the woman who brought me into this world? Across the sound in the blinking beach town she'd rented a cottage in the dunes. Dark pine paneling and thick metal blinds which clicked against the sills, lifted both by the open-windowed breeze and the slow chop of the ceiling fan. Lingering smell of fish, cleaned right in the kitchen sink, then deep fat fried, of her beloved hush puppies, of the lemon wax she scrubbed the furniture with. A front porch overlooking the ocean with bulging and blackened screens.

Here, take these binoculars, she said to me when I entered the house. After the hugs, the pulling me into her softness which, she'd put on a few pounds.

I put the glasses up to my face. The ocean was blurry and gray. A ragged melding of water and sky. I did not know how to focus the lens and I did not see anything at all but I was so glad to be with my mama again, to have been wrapped up in her hug, that I pretended to see porpoises and whales and Glenn the surfer catching the tsunami-sized break of his dreams and hell, to make her happy, the *Pinta*, the *Niña*, and the *Santa María*.

It was true that the view from the porch of the beach cottage was far better than what she'd see from our porch at home, which was the front yard littered with Tank's sand-hauling trucks and dozers, various leaky soccer balls, holes dug by sleepy dogs; a swamp to the left where possums clung to tree tops and the soggy ground was filthy with moccasins and even red-black-yellow, won't-harm-a-fellow corn snakes and evil twin, red-yellow-black, stay-way-back coral snakes which were beautifully banded but deadly, thus the rhyme which Tank could recite well before his ABCs because we knew how he treasured beauty over danger and would certainly have tried to pick one up and pet it if we'd not beat it into him, how dangerous they were; a patchy pine forest to the right where we boys built forts and Carter went sometimes with a bucktoothed neighbor boy named William Tyndall Grice to smoke butts; and in back a big fallow field which was only pleasant in the fall when the stalks turned brown and their raspy cough was brung on sweetly by the breeze.

But even with the help of binoculars all I could see was grayness, blurriness, bleakness, loneliness, okay I'll stop.

What do you see, baby?

I told her, Dolphins. I said, Hey, look, one of those Wind-surfers!

She hugged me from behind and asked was I hungry.

Lying on that bench on the bulkhead I was damn near dying from hunger, thirst, and generalized nastiness of attire.

I could eat if you're having something but you don't have to go to any trouble.

She laughed her what-are-you-talking-about, trouble! laugh and took me inside and went in a back bedroom and came out with a man's T-shirt big on me but clean and smelling of detergent rather than sweat, road grime, Frosty's grill, my sister's cig smoke, probably a little remnant Tank pee, the Mexican's vehicle, booze fumes from Landers, and an odor somewhere between fried seafood and sulfur which I put down to just Bulkhead. I did not ask her whose shirt is this? I did not do or say anything or behave any way which might bring on in her mind boredom or otherwise cause her to put me out. Yes ma'am, no ma'am, thank you please. If you want me to stay I will be perfect, no worries, no trouble, no lip. Without my little brother to look after I was a different person. I had for one thing patience. I believe all those years of taking care of them had built up such reserves of patience that I could, well shy of them, put up with six solid months of someone's most trying bullshit. I was a battery left charging, never used until the storm knocked out the whole county. Light in this world, in this world, this world.

I did not ask her whose shirt but I wondered. You know I bygod wondered who wore it before me.

It was just a blue T-shirt bought obviously at a surf shop, a border of what looked like Hawaiian leis running down one side. Nothing my God-bless-him daddy would have worn. He favored work clothes though not like the Mario I wore — he ripped off the name patches, left ghosts of names, a darker oval where the rest of the shirt had faded from much laundering. He had this one favorite T-shirt he got at the National Hollerin' Contest at Spivey's Corner the first year they held it, before it got big-time and the hippie college kids started driving down from Chapel Hill with their pot and their Hacky Sacks. My mother made like she hated the shirt but of course she loved it to death when he wore it which was nearly every day. She just had to pick. On the porch she sat on the bottom step and he held her in place with his knees. But she wanted to be there. She looked radiant rather than trapped. Whose shirt was this, I thought but did not say.

She hadn't asked me anything about Tank, Carter, or my daddy.

On the water I heard voices. Party people on a yacht. I sat up and saw lights way out across almost to the blinking beach town where in my mother's cottage I sat down at the Formica bar separating the kitchen from the rest of the one not-bedroom room. My mother grilled a cheese sandwich and boiled some white corn. She fixed me a ginger ale which bubbled in its glass. My stomach ached deeply, I thought at first from hunger but do you know what it was in fact from?

The questions she had not asked, my mama, about her other children, about her husband, about bygod me and what I was doing there.

The cheese sizzled. The ginger ale bubbled. I had left both my brothers behind. So had she done the same damn thing. Therefore we were walled off in this place together. What we shared was liable to take us in one of two directions: make us talk about nothing but, or go hard the other way: anything but. My natural inclination would be to get behind door number one, because to me, see, it feels better to confess than it does to deny but I was sitting there eating a grilled cheese sandwich and twirling my ear of white corn in a lake of salty butter fixing to eat it too and my mama had yet to say one word about anyone but me which led me to believe had it been Carter (aka Archie Bell) showing up at her duneside getaway instead of me, hell, my name would never have come up either. You'd think it would, sort of naturally. But it wouldn't of because instead of tell me how's everybody, is Carter getting along okay in school (because he mixed his letters up and therefore hated to read though that boy could tighten up on some arithmetic) and is Tank putting on weight (because he only liked to eat string cheese, Cheerios and Funyuns from Frosty's), she said, They saw some turtles laying eggs ashore the other day and one of them weighed close to four hundred pounds, and We had Hurricane Ida down here in late September but I came out all right, I just lost some shingles. These were things that might of interested Tank, hurricanes and monster washed-ashore turtles,

but I wasn't interested in any of that. She'd forgot how to talk
to me if she ever did know in the first place. What I wanted
to hear out of her mouth was what I'd come all this way for:
why she'd left, how she did it because she loved us, how I was
now that I had left them behind also terrific at love.

Somebody had a hold of my leg. I jerked up off my mama's
barstool. It was a Bulkhead policeman, straddling a bygod
bicycle.

"Get your ass up," he said. "This is a public park, not a
flophouse."

I said I never mistook it for a flophouse and besides I
wasn't flopping.

"This park is closed," he said. "It's three o'clock in the
morning and this park has *been* closed." He pointed to a sign.
POSTED: PARK HOURS, 8 AM TO 11 PM. I started to say, Well you
can read, that's better than Carter, but can you do the
Tighten Up? I decided right then that I missed Carter. I'd
been hard on him. Daddy cut his ear off. He mixed his letters up. He also had something in him made him bored eas-
ily. Except one thing about that I didn't understand: he
could watch *Road Runner* for hours, or could before daddy
golf-clubbed the TV, and it never bored him. *Road Runner*,
if you asked me, was the boringest show, and very aggravat
ing. It was the opposite of entertaining to see how much the
coyote and Road Runner love to mess with each other. What
happened in the first place to make them do each other like
they do? History as usual goes begging. To me the worst thing
about *Road Runner* was the laziness of the dude who drew it.

I hesitate to call him an artist. Over and over he drew the same old rock, the same cactus. It didn't matter whether there was Acme Explosives involved, or a anvil, or a highway painted on the sheer rock face of a mountain to mislead Road Runner, you were going to be staring at that same-ass cactus.

"What are you *on*, boy?" asked the policeman. I said to the Bulkhead bicycle policeman, "I ain't on shit. If you want to catch somebody under a influence you best go after Landers."

He was trying to look menacing from the get-go but he got especially aggressive after I mentioned Landers. Flushed, big-breathed, put his hand on his bygod gun. He had me up off that bench and spread-eagled against a tree before the name Landers got blown off by a breeze. I supposed Landers won't exactly the name to drop to a Bulkhead cop, bicycle or otherwise, and that I ought not to have probably cussed the old boy, though I did not know that cussing a cop or stating the name of a known criminal would result in arrest. I guess I was too busy waiting on my mama to ask after my brothers and daddy to get right inside what they call the moment.

He cuffed my hands. He tightened the cuffs to where I had to ask Archie Bell to back off, I needed loose, not tight. He called for backup which I was wondering how he was going to haul me in on his bicycle.

He read me my rights.

You have the right to a record player, he said. The right to tighten up on that organ, bass, guitar, drums. You have the right to get right inside whatever moment you want or need to, use whatever sweet song will take you there, to avoid that same-ass cactus which, harmless though it may seem when it flashes past the road runner, is a deadly factor in many a wasted life. You have the right to get on board that train, the right to leave behind your baggage and just climb on board. You have the right to leave, the right to get good at love.

"What did I do?"

"The charge is loitering, vagrancy, resisting arrest."

"I never resisted any arrest."

"Also suspicion of other illegal activities associated with your buddy Landers who is a suspect in several unsolved crimes."

"I don't even know Landers."

"You damn sure know how to drop his name for not knowing somebody."

"I just met him walking down the street. I'm not even from this town."

"Tell it all to somebody who's going to give a damn."

Who would that be? I wondered.

A cop car showed up, blue lit, brakes squealing. I started to ask what all the fuss was about but I was aware of how sensitive these cops were because I knew them from the school bus. They were the ones who could dish it all day long, talk all grades of trash about your mama and your high waters but give it back to them and they turn sputtering and bullified. I knew everyone from the school bus—the entire spectrum of humanity rode my Moody Loop bus, the girls I'd never get with, the pure loyal ones and the I'd-do-my-husband's-best-friend sluts, the future lawyers and cops and the video-game-loving nerds, the druggies and the drunks. I could look at them and see them in ten years' time. I could see all this despite the sound track constantly blasting in my inner ear.

I rode in silence to the so-called City Complex, which was brand-new and bland as a office park. I spoke when spoken to. It was a while before anyone spoke to me. A street-clothed cop sat me down at a desk and asked me questions. I told him the exact God's truth. That I was down here looking my mama and I stopped to ask this guy Landers where the Promise Land was and he promised to show me then tricked me into breathing some half-ass neither car nor truck to life which obviously he stole.

"He didn't steal it, it's his," said Streetclothes. "He's not supposed to be driving it if he's had a drink, which Landers is always messed up on something." He explained to me how this Landers had a problem drinking and driving and how the judge had ordered this contraption put in his car measuring his alcohol levels and all this time I thought it was magic. I felt stupid. Babies say mama. I wanted to go home. They'd get me for blowing to life a butt-ugly vehicle that might of for all I know run over a little girl on a Barbie bike.

It occurred to me to wonder why I would care to find my mother if she had no more sense than to stay in Bulkhead. Perhaps they would find her and throw her in jail for being my mother since I was being held in connection to a crime committed by a man who had tricked me into cranking his hybrid. Bulkhead being the sort of place where guilt by association is a literal letter-of-the-law-type situation.

In that case I had better not say her name.

Streetclothes was on my side, I could tell. If he'd had something to prove he would have worn his uniform. Also he took one look at me and knew I wasn't any colleague of Landers. I was just this smelly kid in a purloined shirt.

"Mario, what's your last name, buddy?" He had gotten some forms out of a file cabinet but he'd pushed them aside. He was looking at me like he really wanted to know my name.

"My name is really not even Mario," I told him because he was as kind as the kindly Mexican. "I just borrowed this shirt because I spent the night out on a fishing pier."

"Oh, okay," he said, as if this made some sense to him. "You say you're looking for your mom?"

"Yes," I said. Mom. Babies don't even know what that means.

"Say she stays down in the Promise Land?"

"Yes, sir," I said. I'd remembered Sheriff Deputy Rex saying you always addressed an officer of the law as "sir."

"Where at down there?"

"I don't know. See, that's how come I happened to run into that Landers. He was leaning against a wall down by that pool room—"

"He'd 'bout have to lean," said Streetclothes.

"I walked by and asked which way was the Promise Land and that's when he tricked me into cranking his car or whatever by blowing in the tube."

"Well, that ain't no crime. What were you doing when-ever Officer Weaver who brung you in found you?"

I was having dinner with my mama. She was asking me did I want some ice cream. We sat at the bar. I wanted her to put on some Aretha like she used to do at home but that was our old home, she didn't live there anymore. Maybe she'd never lived there. Maybe she'd always been like she was to me then, talking to me like I was some baby. We had a hur-ricane! Four-hundred-pound sea turtles! Okay, I'll have some ice cream. You asked me to call you the moment I got here. Now here I am and you act like you hardly know me.

"Listening to some music," I said.

Streetclothes looked at me strangely. He'd been standing there when they brought me in and had watched me empty my pockets. He'd seen the nothing but nickels and pennies change, the wad of tissue I kept to wipe Tank's dirty mouth and a few pieces of retard candy I was hiding from Tank.

"In my head," I explained. "You know how you do."

"Un-hunh." He had this look on his face. I'd seen the same look on Sheriff Deputy Rex. Like he wanted to feel sorry for you but would just as soon be involved in a high speed pursuit as taking care of the children of a sorryass and his run-off wife.

"Well, where's your daddy at?"

I named my town.

"He know you've run off?"

"He knows now."

"Other words, you didn't ask his permission to come down here and visit your mama?"

"No, sir, not really."

"How come you didn't tell him? Don't you think he's going to be worried?"

I stared at my shoes, which still had their laces. This must of meant they weren't going to lock me up. They take your laces so you won't hang yourself. I loved my daddy, my daddy was a good man. I hated to talk about his situation to a stranger. But I did not want them to send me back to him. I was just getting good at love. People aren't born with any natural aptitude in that direction. If they were, what would be the source of all the sweet songs? We're defined by what we lack. The shortfall will force you to make up a dance called the Tighten Up. Say we were all born knowing how to adequately love. Turn on the radio and there'd be nothing to listen to but that old monotone man out of Chadbourne quotes the going rates per pound for hogs, or some white-bread preacher trying to make you feel worse than you already do for tuning in to his white-bread ass.

"My daddy's sick."

"What kind of sick is he?"

"Sick in the head." I pointed to my temple for effect.

"Uh-hunh. So you don't stay with him?"

"I did until two days ago."

"What happened two days ago?"

Then I felt trapped. Like I had run off in the woods and

gotten myself good and lost and was about going to have to fight my way out of it instead of stay there and wait to be discovered which was my natural inclination. I did not know what had happened back home. I had not been thinking about it, or about poor Carter or Tank either. Just me and my mama sitting at the bar, grilled cheese and buttered corn, sea turtles and hurricanes, iced tea and Fig Newtons.

"My daddy went off."

"You mean he went off and left y'all alone?"

"No, he didn't leave. He's there, he just ain't there." I tapped my temple again. I made sure to act bored when I did so, like it had happened so many times before. That same-ass cactus.

"Okay. And did somebody come get him, take him to get some help?"

"I don't know. I left."

"How did you get down here?"

I looked at a spot behind my interviewer's head and stuck my thumb out, exhibit B. It seemed like I was communicating mostly with gestures. Soon I'd be down to shrugs.

"How come you didn't just call your mama on the phone?"

"I don't believe her number's listed."

"You don't believe, or you checked and it ain't?"

"Well, sir, I didn't think calling her up and announcing my arrival would be the best strategy."

"Okay, I hear you. You were wanting to take her by surprise."

"Yes, sir."

"Either that works or it don't," he said, as if this could not be said of most anything. "What's your mama's name?"

She's the one named me after him. She must have known. Babies don't call their mamas full given Christian names. Her name is Joyce. Joyce Dunn. But I have never heard her called such a thing. I felt myself unraveling, tried to tighten up. Flatly I said her name. Streetclothes wrote it down, leaned over, pulled a phone book from a bottom drawer. He licked his finger and paged loudly through it while I felt myself unraveling, tried to tighten up.

"Nope," he said, holding the book away as if he'd forgot his glasses. "Could she of got remarried?"

"She loved us so she had to leave, " I said. "She could not stay because she loved us so much it would of killed her."

"Okay," he said. "Who's we?"

"Me. Tank and Carter. Also Angie but she left too."

"How long's your mama been gone?"

I am no good at calendars. I was tired of words. I shrugged, exhibit C.

"So your mama and daddy, they ain't in contact?"

I wanted to say that I heard my daddy talking to her all the time and that he sang to her all the time too. Whatever song he was listening to at the time? It was sent directly from his heart to hers. That's the thing about music if it's any damn good. It's like it's coming straight out of your heart, not from some boxy console record player.

"Okay. I take it you don't know the answer to that one. I

guess we'll have to try harder to find her then. We got ways other than looking her up in the phone book."

"I imagine you do," I said. I was glad my fate rested in the hands of Streetclothes. But I was all of a sudden so hungry my stomach cramped. I doubled over, holding it.

"You need to go to the bathroom?"

I thought of Tank, how much he hated it when I asked him did he have to go.

I said I did. He led me down the hall to it. There were some rights and lefts. He told me how to get back. But I took a wrong turn. There was some plate glass and, outside it the sidewalk, the streetlights set to blink until dawn. There was Bulkhead and my mama who he could not locate in his computer because she had done nothing wrong. I went on. But I took a wrong turn. There was the plate glass and, outside it, the sidewalk, the streetlight set to blink until dawn. I stood there with my hands on the door, my fingerprints smudging the glass. Then I realized where I was and lifted a corner of Mario to wipe clean the prints. I was wiping still when Streetclothes come up behind me.

"There you are," he said. "Cleaning up?"

"Somebody missed a spot."

"Get lost?"

But I took a wrong turn.

"Follow me then," he said. There was something different in his voice. Back at his desk two or three men hung about, staring at me. I could tell from their faces that my status had changed during the time I had been gone. Fat Frosty must of turned me in for running off with his tank of gas. They were fixing to make me remove my laces.

"You never told me your name, did you?"

"You never asked. Fat Frosty don't know me, though."

"Who's Fat Frosty?"

Then I thought: Something happened to Carter. More than lost an earlobe.

"What happened to Carter?"

"Hold up. Who's Carter?"

Then it was, Oh you idiot! The only one who knows you're down here is Angie. She doesn't want Tank hanging around cramping her foul-mouthed style what it is. So she notified the authorities. No telling what kind of crime she'd hang on me.

"Angie's friends use marijuana," I said.

"You got to stop talking about people I never heard of. My wife does that same thing. At least explain to me who these people are to you."

Then it was the end of the list. I did not know anyone else. My daddy would not yet be back on. Carter would have been glad to see me gone, frankly. I didn't always do him so good.

"Anybody else could take care of you?" he said. "Aunts? Grandparents? Neighbors?"

Then I understood. He had talked to her while I was gone. They had ways of finding people other than the phone book. It did not take her long to make her wishes known. About the time it took me to wipe my prints off the plate glass. To go to the bathroom.

"Son," he said, and I did not like Streetclothes saying that. Especially because even though she was dead to me from that point on no matter what he said I didn't care to hear him insinuate I wasn't hers nor my daddy's. I was not his son. I was still theirs even though one was sick and the other, dead.

"How did she die?" I asked him.

He tried to look like he wouldn't of rather been in a stake-out. He was doing the best he could. I could tell he might have gone into law enforcement to help people at the start of it, though that wasn't what kept him in it now. But there was some left over from when he was just starting out.

"We can't make her take you, okay? We can see to it you get some shelter but the one thing we can't do is make somebody feel the way they ought to feel," he said. "I sure as hell wish we could."

Have you ever tried to stop your mind from going where it believes it ought to go? Like a dog digging a sleeping hole up under a shade bush, my mind kept seeking out that cold secret sand.

"In a house fire you say? She died in a house fire?"

Streetclothes looked at my dirty shirt. "It'd be a lot better on all of us, I swear, if we could just tell somebody to act right and that be the end of it," he said.

"Well," I said. I swallowed. It staved off the tears so I did it again. Then I just sat there swallowing, the fire crackling in her basement. Down there so close to the ocean she said it would fill with water before you could even shovel out the sand. But she was wrong: she had a basement down in the

Promise Land and it was filled with things people thought they were through with which still had some good use left in them. People'll dump perfectly good shit down a bygod ravine. A basement or attic is filled with items which have whole other lives left in them. People just get bored is what it is. They just give up. Or they say I'm tired of fighting with this toaster, I'm just going to chuck it in the basement or up under the attic eaves and get me a brand-new one. Watch it sink down in the thick pink blanket of insulation, the sucking mud behind the furnace. Whole chicken houses filled with items fallen prey to somebody got good and bored. Oh the waste in this world. All I wanted was a space below and up above me so I could keep it clean of the kind of castoffs known to clog such spaces and turn them into Deadly Firetraps. See, it's hazardous to your health, abandoning things, allowing boredom to take hold. It's that same-ass cactus.

Some old boy wearing a T-shirt, blue with a Hawaiian lei border, drops by to visit in her house down in the Promise Land. You got to go outside to smoke, Ronnie, she says to him when he shakes a Vantage from a crumpled pack. But it's cold outside or spitting rain or just general Bulkhead fish-gill gray. He waits until she's in the kitchen cooking to cranked up Aretha, then slips down the basement steps. He'll be goddamned if he'll stand out in the elements just for something as wispy as smoke. At the foot of the stairs he lights up, blows smoke toward the shadows where there are ass-busted chairs, one-legged tables, light fixtures, and fireplace grates, all of it dusty and tarnished but none of it beyond repair. You don't just up and leave it all behind. Ronnie smokes his smoke. He does not even notice the whole other left behind world lurking inches away in the cool up-underground dog-dug shadows. When he finishes his cig he flicks it in those same-ass shadows. Let's say he decides right then and there to leave, okay? Let's let him leave. She ought not to have had him over there in the first place so we'll clear Ronnie right on out and let my mama lie down on the couch while the cigarette smolders and catches on some prematurely discarded something-another down there which snaps and blisters and all of a sudden busts up in blue dancing flames, sending smoke upstairs to where my mama breathes in those things people ought not to have throwed away in the first place. This is what kills her: lethal inhalation of second chances.

Will you take me by there? I was about to ask him, but I knew there won't nothing to see. Burned to the ground. I saw the lowly residents of the low-lying Promise Land standing around the charred brick and ash. I got up close enough to listen.

"Won't nothing left but the basement."

"I didn't never see her, she worked all the time."

"Somebody said she had children."

"All I ever saw her with was what's-his-name, used to crew for Butterball Midgette."

"She was a pretty gal."

"Y'all didn't know her," I said to the lot of them. I pushed right up among them. "Y'all can't talk about her, she won't even from here."

They all looked at me. I was swallowing to keep from crying. Streetclothes said, Need some water? I said I need to go to the bathroom again. But that wasn't what I needed. I needed to stop seeking out that cold secret sand. I knew I could of stayed there and let them sort it all out. Streetclothes would have done me right. But Sheriff Deputy Rex wasn't a bad man either, it's just his hands were tied and he didn't make the rules and there was paperwork to fill out and they'd have taken me right then and there and made me a Ward of the State and I would never have gotten to see my brothers again. I walked down the hall toward the bathroom. I couldn't hear anything in that building. No sweet horns breaking in the middle of Tighten Up. Maybe that was where I needed to be — some place where the music could not reach me. But it's the worse kind of death, suffocated by the second chances you were too proud or bored or wrongheaded to heed. Oh I was so old. I passed by a hundred cacti. Then I came to a break room. It smelled of microwave popcorn, coffee, and cigarettes. In the refrigerator I found bagged lunches, Tupperwared leftovers. I put it all in a trash bag I found under the sink which I slung over my shoulder like a hobo. I read myself my rights: You have the right to leave behind your baggage and just climb on board. You have the right to leave, the right to get good at love.

SEVEN

THEN I WAS NOT listening to the song in my head, which leaving Bulkhead was the Staple Singers, "I'll Take You There." I wanted to be like Carter: could take or leave the sound track, could choreograph a half-time show-stopper to "Tighten Up," could pretend to even be Archie Bell, but knew inside it was only a song, just entertainment, nothing to live your life by. I wanted to be like Carter even when Mavis Staples started singing about Heaven or a place she knew where everybody's happy and Pop Staples winged in with some righteous gospel chords and that bass line slapped along making sure your ass and hips knew that white people all the way back to the Pilgrims and forward to the First Prez crowning the choicest hill in town had got religion all wrong. I would have believed in anything for the three and half minutes that song lasted: Heaven, Carter, bygod Bulkhead, a ark with two of everything up in it, my daddy's goodness.

Well, no, not that. It's because of my daddy that I always

had a song in my head and craved basement attic crawl space. Because of him I left my brothers and sought out my mother. Walking through the backstreets of Bulkhead, clinging to the yards and trees in case Streetclothes was out looking for me, I thought that these songs my daddy put in my head were nothing but moods I did not have the depth to summon on my own. And to think I was walking around judging everybody else for not grooving to some tunes. Come to find out I was a robot, a computer, every emotion programmed. You could drop quarters down my throat and punch up some selections and I'd feel whatever Otis, Sly, Aretha, Reverend Al *made* me feel. I damn near sat down and died whenever this thought hit me, for the scariest revelation you can have is that you cannot truly feel a thing.

I wanted to be like Carter, like Angie even, bless her goddamn motherfucking foul-mouthed self.

Tank, Tank, it's not too late for you, buddy. It's too late for Mario, Tank. I'm leaving out of Bulkhead with a sack of Tupperwared po-lice leftovers on my back. I don't love my daddy anymore, I can't feel jack but whatever Mavis and Pop tell me too. Right now though they're saying they'll take me there, Tank. I'm going wherever they lead.

Cops like leftover lasagna with extra meat sauce. Also they like meat loaf. They like some pizza. Vegetables don't seem big on the menu of things craved by cops.

I ate in a little shelter someone had built for schoolkids waiting on the bus. It was dark out and quiet except for a paper man moving up the side street, his blinkers on, chucking plastic-wrapped news onto dew-dampened lawns. Each wet thwack echoed in my head. Still I ate and ate. Then I felt sick, all that meaty cop food in a stomach that had shrunk to the size of a peach pit. I near about threw up in the bus shelter. I lay out on the bench moaning. That's Bulkhead for you, me lying on some bench, about to hurl, breaking some Bulkhead law while cops searched for me on bygod bicycles. Above the pines the sky turned pink. Mavis was fixing to take me there. I got up to follow along.

Out on the highway a trucker stopped for me not three minutes after I set up on the misty shoulder. I'll take you there, sang the air brakes. You'll be wanting to know what the inside of the truck looked like but Tank I'm telling you I didn't pay one bit of attention. A crazy kind of fear gripped me: She'd taken you back to our daddy. Who was still way off. Who was going to hurt you too.

The truck driver tried to talk to me, Mavis sang to me, Pop Staples plucked celestial chords for me but all I could think about was nothing. Still sick from all that food on an empty stomach and to top it off was the notion that my mama had gone off and died all alone in a fire which was and is still my worst fear, that I'll end up dying all alone in an empty chicken house stuffed with used appliances. But I could not make myself feel all you're supposed to feel after your mother dies in a house fire. I could not pay any attention to the inside of the truck, Tank, and the driver I'm sure wished he'd never stopped for my mute, stupefied ass.

I could think about nothing. The music was playing, taking me there, but it was just background, like it always was for normal people.

That I could sit up in that truck and have all these thoughts competing for time in my head and think about nothing, well, that got away with me. Robot, computer, cyborg, alien. I wondered if everybody already knew it about me anyway. If it was whispered behind my back so often it was if a breeze followed me around rustling leaves in the trees I passed. Lifting bangs off girl's foreheads, the news that there ain't nobody home up inside Joel Junior Dunn.

I meant to say Mario. From then on that's what I was going to go by.

The piney woods sped by. Occasionally we came up on some pickup dragging ass along with its turn signal blinking though there won't nowhere to turn for miles but some pulpwood trails. I'd look down at people which I did because I physically *could* do. It didn't make me feel any less an alien or soothe my stomach though I did not stop myself from still doing it.

I wondered where was Landers. He was about the caliber person I ought to of been hanging out with seeing as how I could not feel any more than a dope addict morning noon and night messed up on some kind of dope.

"Where you want to be let out at?" said the trucker. It was the first time he'd said jack to me in miles and miles. Mavis was taking me, leading me by the hand.

"Bottomsail," I said. Maybe I sounded irritated but I had told him that once already when I first got in.

"You best not expect me to turn off this highway."

"You can just let me off at that drawbridge."

"Was that a whole sentence you just said?"

I said, "My mother died in a house fire. I just found out."

"Damn," he said. Then: "O Lord."

I said, "I'll take the former and to hell with the latter."

He looked at me like he was fixing to call me son and I said I didn't want to talk about it. The only reason I told him in the first place was to shut him up. But he did not shut up.

"Where you going to now?" he said.

"To tell my sister and little brother."

"They with your pa?"

"My pa is probably in Dix Hill by now." I didn't need to explain Dix Hill because everybody down east knows it's where they stick nuts, retards, and habitual drunks.

He said, "I'll drive you over the bridge."

"You don't have to."

"Naw," he said, "I'll drive you."

I watched the sparkling yachts as we crossed the bridge. Then we were on the beach road and he was taking me door to door, except there wasn't any door on either side, he just felt sorry for me and carried me right up to the pier where once we saw the magic caster, slept sprawled out on the slats, and went down on some sausage dogs.

I searched the parking lot for my daddy's pickup but it was gone, gone.

The trucker lifted his ass up off the seat. He pulled out his western-style wallet. I admired the stitching. He handed me a twenty.

"No thank you, sir, you already give me a ride."

"I'm thankful my mama and daddy are still here," he said. "You take it. I'm not going to tell you what to do because you seem to me like you're doing all right but you might ought to learn to give God a shot."

I smiled good-bye and thank you very much you're so very kind at the trucker and let myself down out of that truck into the parking lot.

I walked out on the pier. Maybe the magic caster was still there, maybe he'd gone home and come back, maybe he was a fixture. Surely you don't tighten up that much on the rod and reel by rocking all day long on a metal porch glider. He was in permanent residence. I'd be so happy to see him. Where's Little Man at? he'd say, talking about you, Tank. I'd tell him you were taking a nap. Then I would try to pay him back what he spent on us out of the trucker's twenty though he'd take a look at me in my same-old Mario and jeans, my hair greasy as mop water, and he would not take my cash, no way.

He wasn't out there. I sat on his same-ass bench for a long time staring up the coast to Bulkhead. I was trying not to listen to Mavis. I wasn't even sure that song was about Heaven—as much grunting and moaning there was, it seemed like some other kind of ecstasy—but wherever she was wanting to take me I was wanting to go, and it was distracting me, I needed to think what next. I was older than the magic caster, sitting there wrinkled and shivering on his very bench.

Twenty minutes later I was standing in front of Angie's scummy apartment. The screen door was ajar. Mosquitoes were letting themselves in and out. I could smell the spilled beer and bong water in the carpet from near about back at the beach road. Tank sat on the floor in front of the television playing a video game. He looked up at me when I knocked and went back to his screen. Wasn't no more than him dragging his eyes across my face. Everybody already knew it about me anyway. A breeze followed me around rustling leaves in the trees I passed, lifting bangs off foreheads: He can't feel a thing, it whispered. He's no more human than that video game's got you sucked in same as he will.

Even before my daddy golf-clubbed the evil infiltrators out of the television set we would never have spent our days sitting in front of it trying to shoot mutants or racing spaceships. We'd rather play our records or visit in the woods near our house a chicken house stuffed with used appliances. In a corner we'd grouped some stoves and fridges together and had our own short-order grill. I'll take you there. I let myself in the apartment. Tank slapping at buttons, twisting a joy stick, not looking up. Who could blame him? There were empty beer bottles and heaping ashtrays on every inch of the coffee table. Tank in the same clothes I last saw him in. His hair all woody-woodpeckered. Not looking at me. First his sister then his mama then his daddy now his brother. I could not blame him for taking refuge in a Nintendo or whatever

you call it. This was Angie's way of stepping up to the bygod
plate I reckon, leaving him alone with a joystick all day long.
I saw what I wanted to see in the way she hugged him after
she thought he'd drowned. But I craved attic basement crawl
space my mama and it made me blind. Did I actually in fact
assume Angie would have purchased with her cigarette
money matching striped shirt and little blue shorts for Tank,
that his hair would be wetcombed instead of coxcombed,
that he'd be sitting quietly in a circle of lamplight in a spot-
less living room reading *Rikki-Tikki-Tavi* or *Wind in the Wil-
lows* and that when I appeared in line with the mosquitoes to
gain entry into the apartment he would hop up and run to
the door and jump into my arms?

What I come back to was a different Tank. Not-Tank.
Lawrence I guess I ought to call him from here on out. That
being his name.

I'd thought I'd lost him and everybody else, forever. I
should have stuck with Streetclothes. He'd let me stay in his
new ranch house out on the edge of Bulkhead, bordering the
soybean and cabbage fields. His wife would keep that house
icebox cold as it would sit out in the fields without a tree in
sight, baking in the Bulkhead sun. Skinny people are meaner,
but big people like it nearly freezing inside. Sometimes we'd
need gloves to open the coolers in Frosty's, so cold did he
keep that place. When Streetclothes and the wife would
drive off to work I'd set up shop in his metal storage shed and
watch the crop dusters daredevil down onto the fields and
spray their poisonous potion and jerk it just in time back up

into the sky. At night the mosquito man would come chugging down the street, leaving his clouds of DDT for me to watch disperse over the crabgrassy yards of the neighborhood. Mrs. Streetclothes would fix me some meaty cop food for dinner and whatever was left I would tupperware for school the next day. Maybe the kindly Mexican would send for me to stay with him and his family down Guadalajara way. I'd sell fruit by the roadside and smile at everything I didn't understand. I would get with a sweet brown Mexican girl and we'd climb in a hammock in a dark corner of a windowless room when everyone was gone off to work in the fields and we'd make the same noises Mavis makes in a song that might just not be about that kind of Heaven at all, which is why I love it, for the borderline way it brings together the inside and the outside, sacred and the get damn down.

How to get him out of this trance, Mavis?

"Hey, Tank," I said.

Nothing. Gunfire, squealing tires, spaceship noises.

"Tank. Hey, Tank."

Nada, which is kindly Mexican for he didn't say shit to me.

"Okay, well, I'll just take a seat and wait for you to finish."

I sat on the couch. There was a pillow and a ratty thermal blanket bunched up at one end. I wondered if Tank had to stay up until everyone left.

"Y'all have a party last night?"

Guns, spaceships, stuff exploding loudly.

"Okay, I'm just going to talk then," I said.

I told him about the Mexican. I described the mariachi music and even sang a little but I doubt he heard me over the commotion. I told him I got off in Bulkhead. I didn't say what for. I wasn't about to tell him what for and what happened until he was at least looking me in the eye. While I talked I went over and flipped through the CDs to see if I could find something we liked. My daddy refused to get a CD player. What would I do with my records? he said. He said if we was to move to a spaceship then maybe he'd get one. But first he'd at least try to haul his boxy cabinet stereo on board. It's about six or seven feet long and heavy as Frosty's coffin will one day be.

All Angie's surfer boys had was some heavy metal. I know it's all just personal taste but I can't see how anyone can listen to some Megadeath. What does that even mean, megadeath? Like you died really big? Or a bunch of times? Metallica, that sounds like the color Landers would choose to paint his hybrid vehicle.

"Landers and the hybrid whistle, by Mario Dunn," I announced. "Once I happened to be walking down the street in Bulkhead." (Here I heaped scorn on Bulkhead in a big and quite eloquent though biased way. "The place smelled like megadeath." Also: "The buildings were painted a peeling metallica.") You wonder what I was doing there? Well, I was trying to locate a particular neighborhood."

I looked down at Tank, who still had not looked at me, and it made me mad. I might of left him but it was not quite twenty-four hours and think of all I'd done for him prior, and consider also how I'd come back to lead him out of there. So I reached down and grabbed that joy stick out of his hand which brought an end to his joy. He went to wailing.

It made me wonder why I even came back: Angie's apartment filled with evidence of kids trying to live on their own like grown-ups but wasting away every night getting stupid, no music to listen to except (thank you, Jesus) Mavis up in my head, Tank in the short time I had been gone, technically less than a day, addicted to video games. The evil forces had overtaken both of them. I might of hated my daddy for being like he was but I will tell you one thing, if he hadn't of gone off he'd not of let this happen. Some would maybe say he'd ruined us or at least me by depriving us of television and video games and all the latest high-tech toys and instead spinning records that were a good, some of them, thirty or forty years old if they were a day, black-washing us into believing that white boys from England might could master a twelve-bar blues (though mostly they just turned their amplifiers up real loud) but the true sound track of our lives rose out of the very land we tread upon, the fields we passed on our way to school each day, swarming now with kindly Mexicans but once tended entirely by the forebears of the singers we treasured, and the churches, half-finished or unadorned, heated with nothing but sheet-metal trash burners, you'd see back in the pine groves, and of course the county jail and the low-ceilinged, no-windowed cinder-block jukes that fed that jailhouse, sprinkled throughout the county and down the side streets of town, two to three for every church.

Just take me by the hand, Tank. Let me lead the way.

True I sometimes wandered out of range and lost the signal myself and yes I sometimes, left to my own half-formed judgment, strayed or was seduced by songs that lacked the purity of my daddy's favorites, like my brief flirtation with Motown, a label my daddy didn't much care for because, he said, with all due respect for Mr. Barry Gordy who as a businessman deserved his props, it made black music palatable to white people, lightening it up so it would cross over to the pop charts. My daddy when he was on could be an I-got-there-first snob. He could lecture for hours on the production quality of Motown versus anything out of Memphis or Muscle Shoals, the former being slick and given to the latest technology and the latter being sloppy in the way that perfect things just naturally are—filled with human error, the fuckups there to honor not Allah like the imperfection in the carpet but Jesus-I-don't-think-so, though if anyone ever came close to convincing me it was bygod Mavis callin' Mercy, telling her daddy to play on it, play on it, hollerin Whoa (to which I whispered, Whoa) All right (to which I hollered, Well, okay, all right).

I didn't realize I was hollering All Right until I looked down and saw Tank staring.

"What's all right?"

"Just listening to a little Mavis and Pop."

"'Respect Yourself'?"

"Up next. Right now we've got 'I'll Take you There.'"

I thought I had him, but he was still smarting from my

leaving him. It was going to take more than the mention of the Staples to win him back.

"Let's go eat," I said. "Then let's run by the Dollar Store and get some candy."

"I want my mama," he said.

"I told you about that, Tank."

"Well, *you* got to go see her."

"Who said?" But I knew damn well who.

"Angie said. She said that's where you run off to, see Mama."

I didn't want to tell him. It wasn't time. But I wanted to tell Angie. She did not deserve my lie—she'd tried to warn me, she'd told the truth before I left out of there for Bulkhead, *She don't want to see us*, she'd said—but I was mad at her for leaving and mad at her for telling Tank where I'd gone and big-time pissed at her for not stepping up to the plate, leaving him all day long in her smelly apartment with its centerfolds from surfing magazines and beer posters Scotch-taped to the walls and its empties all over the place.

"Let's go get something to eat."

"I want McDonald's."

Oh Tank. I know a place.

"There ain't any McDonald's down here."

"Then I ain't hungry."

"I'll buy you a toy at the Dollar Store."

This worked enough to get him out of the house at least. He wanted to go by the Breezeby for lunch but I was not yet ready to face my sister and besides I was jealous that he wanted anything to do with her, suspicious as I was of the way she treated him. Sometimes when my daddy had been off for a while and then climbed shakily back on, my mama treated him like he'd returned from bloody combat. She spoiled him. Grilled us steaks, twice-baked some potatoes, boiled some green beans. She was no kind of cook but this was her one meal, welcome back, daddy, won't you stay with us awhile? Callin' mercy, mercy, mercy. We'd eat out on the porch if it was not mosquito season. Then my daddy would put on James Brown *Live at the Apollo 1962* side one with the crazy intro listing all the songs and the surf guitar and horn prelude and crank that bad boy up so loud you could stand in the bathroom in front of the toilet and not hear the blessed stream hit the water. Then he and his bride would disappear into the bedroom and lock the door behind them. Angie and Carter would sometimes put their ear up to the door but all they could hear was JB knocking them out the aisles of the Apollo. I doubted Angie had the decency or the aforethought to crank up even Megadeath before her or Glenn or whoever she had got with since I'd been gone (perhaps the massive Termite had reappeared on the scene) went at their nighttime lights-out bidness. I hate to admit it but thinking about this led me to imagine myself with that smoke-for-brains hip-huggered Carla. I was singing some Sam Cooke to that girl and it was working as she had been subjected to a steady diet of REO Speedwagon which beats me what a REO Speedwagon even is and she was swaying to my tune, slipping out of her halter and then inching down those huggers and kicking them off finally to shimmy out of these lovely low-cut panties when Tank said, I'm hungry, Joel Junior, where we going to eat?

My name is Mario. I will take you there.

We walked down the beach to the pier. They had a grill built out over the dunes. We sat at the counter and ate cheeseburgers and fries and drank Mr. Pibb while the counterman told us and an old retired navy man about the time there was a grease fire started in the kitchen of the rival pier (because he claimed their fries were so greasy if you were to throw an order in the ocean they'd cause a slick bigger than that Exxon *Valdez*) and a land breeze fanned the fire and drove it out over the pier where it continued ablaze, trapping twenty-some-odd fishermen out at the dead end where some surfers who had been banned by Bottomsail law from surfing within five hundred feet of the pier paddled over to jeer and urge the old boys to jump.

Tank listened to this story, his eyes crazy wide.

"I wonder was Glenn one of those surfers," he said.

"Sounds like him."

"Glenn let me look at his dirty magazines."

"That's it," I said. "Come on, we're going to see Angie."

"No, no, Dollar Store, Dollar Store," he said.

"Okay," I said. I put off asking about the magazines until my food digested. It was the only real meal I'd had aside from Tupperwared police leftovers and I was dog tired from nothing but bench sleep. What I really wanted was to curl up in my very own bed. I supposed I had already made up my

mind to go back but I hadn't yet let myself aloud say it or
even totally inside spell it out. It was just a suction pulling
me. Faintly did the signal grow stronger when I strayed away
from the surf and steered Tank westward ho toward the
dunes. Let me let me let me. Then that harmonica riff that
was like jumping off a building and trusting whoever's blowing that harp (Was it old Pop Staples? My daddy, he'd know)
to keep on blowing because the moment he ran out of breath
was the moment I'd drop to my certain death. What they call
a leap of faith. About Jesus I just don't know now. I want
something up there besides my high-up-in-some-hotel mama.
Somebody lining up my rides. I'd let kindly Mexican reign
supreme, Streetclothes, hell, even Landers if he'd clean himself up, unlike Otis I believe in people's ability to change.
Just let me get home and crawl in my bed which after Angie
left I did get my own room, though Tank when he's scared of
the pine needles scraping the shingles or the coral snakes
popping up out of the heating vent at night when he's too
groggy to remember the rhyme we taught him before we
ever bothered with his ABCs has been known to come sliding in my bed. Used to before my sister left in a cloud of
comic-book asterisks, exclamation points, and question marks,
I shared a room with Tank and Carter. They had bunk beds
with wagon-wheel headboards to which they'd bind each
other with my daddy's two ties I not once saw him wear.
Cowboy and Indian, a far healthier for you pursuit than any
video game as it involves the creation in what they call your
mind's eye of that same-ass cactus, tumbleweeds blowing down

the dusty main street of Dodge, swinging saloon doors, give me a sasparillo in a dirty glass. I begged off playing because it was for babies but occasionally I would cameo in the role of high sheriff which I ain't bragging but I feel I brought more integrity to the role of public servant than the preoccupied and often downright mocking Sheriff Deputy Rex.

I let Tank loose in the aisles of the Dollar Store which had not shifted a dust mote since I'd last patronized it. The same Muzak version of James Taylor's "Fire and Rain" leaked like nuclear fallout from the dropped ceiling. Thank God for Mavis. I deliberated over the purchase of a three-pack of Fruit of the Looms for Tank which would leave us with only five dollars to get Tank a toy and us home on, the Dollar Store being in fact a damn lie, most of the stock costing considerably more. Tank chose finally, after I had to suffer through string-only versions of "Dreams" by Fleetwood Mac, "I'm Not in Love," by 10cc, and "Baby, I Love Your Way," by Peter Frampton, a package of green plastic army men.

"You got this same pack at home," I said.

"But I want it."

"We're going home today."

"This," he shouted, shaking it in my face.

"Okay," I said. I was going to pay big-time for leaving him behind. Also I figured he wanted to feel at home until he arrived there safely. Safe seemed the wrong word considering no telling what we'd find when we arrived there. I tuned into Mavis, not wanting to consider what we'd come home to find. I remembered that morning we left Tank and Carter had been playing with their plastic army men up under the bed. That is what he'd been doing when my daddy went off. I'm no shrink but it makes some sense to me that he'd want to take up where he left off. Besides the army men were nearly the only thing he was considering which cost in fact not much over one buck.

We went to the dock on the sound behind the Breezeby to wait for Angie to get off work. It was hot and breezeless and I only wanted to sleep but I did not want to go back to Angie's apartment which made me sad, livid, and itchy all at once and putting aside my own feelings I did not want Tank thumbing that joystick in front of that box. I craved my house on a hill, its basement up under the cool earth, the sweetly simple logic of an overheated dog: dig down to stay cool. Tank set his army men up on the railing and commenced his play-by-play of their epic struggle to rid the world of evil. In turn, Tank-like, I lay facedown on the dock, my nose slotted in the space between slats, smelling the fishy waters of the sound, rooting around in my basement, drifting off toward that space in my head where I don't have to take care of no-body and the music is chosen for me by a DJ I believe to be (even though I hate him) I-love-my: daddy.

I told Tank keep a lookout for Angie when she got off work and an hour later I heard him call out to her. It was cool in-side my basement and Mavis and Pop had moved on to "Re-spect Yourself" and I was about around to where I could do so before Angie came flat-flooting it up the dock, no doubt thinking when she saw me stretched across the boards that

Tank had messed up big time. Maybe killed a man. A conclusion logical if shocking seeing as how she left him alone all day to play video games and allowed her no-count boyfriend to show him porno and I wouldn't be surprised if they did not get him high for their own entertainment.

She stopped dead when she saw it was me. I guess she recognized old sweat-stained Mario, my resilient shell.

"You better fucking wish you were dead," she said.

I pulled myself up all slat-creased and sweaty and this is when she slapped, kicked, and in general reverted to that tomboy self used to beat hell out of all the boys she played H-O-R-S-E and Twenty-one with in the sandy, cone-strewn backyard courts off Moody Loop. I put my hands up to shield her blows and laughed like I always used to when she went physically off. I guess because it was funny to me. Tank wasn't laughing. It got away with him big-time. He wormed his way between us trying to break it up.

"Red-yellow-black, stay way back," I said to him.

"What the fuck?" said Angie. She'd stopped swinging. I looked back at the plate-glass windows of the Breezeby to see the waitstaff, the cooks, the big-haired hostess, and a couple of patrons holding bottles of beer staring at the show.

"Don't tell me you've finally gone off too," she said.

"He is not," said Tank.

"If I were you I'd cool it," I said, pointing to the audience.

"Excellent," she said. "I'm sure they'll fire my ass now."

"You don't want to stay here anyhow."

"You don't get to tell me where to stay. Especially not now, Mr. I'm Just Going to Get Something out of the Truck."

"He went to see Mama," said Tank.

"He sure didn't stay long, did he?" said Angie.

I told Angie I needed to talk to her. Her sneer bled into a smirk.

"Didn't I tell you? What part of she don't want to have anything to do with us is confusing to you?"

"Who?" said Tank.

"Go play with your army men," I told him.

"Who don't want to have anything to do with us?"

"Great," I said to Angie. "See?"

"You'd rather lie to him, obviously. Tell him you'll be back in a minute, got to just get something out of the truck. Do you know he asked for you every ten minutes all fucking night long?"

I looked at Tank. He went back to his army men as if he was ashamed of calling out for me.

"I finally had to let him play video games," said Angie, "just to get him to settle the hell down."

I was so old. Now I'm a baby compared to that moment, out over the sound, in the boiling afternoon sun.

Tank was humming and moving about his army men in seconds. Angie lit a cigarette and said, "What?"

I started talking. Mavis was taking me by the hand. Wherever she was promising to take me it was a far better place than the no d Promise Land, where mamas denied their own offspring to kindly must-have-some-Mexican-blood street-clothed cops.

I described the fire. "I asked him take me by there to see but he said it was nothing left," I said. Burned to the ground. Just some charred bricks and ash.

Angie stood there staring. Her cigarette, stuck in her hand like a sixth finger, smoked like the ruins of my mama's cottage.

She never said a word about it. Just turned and walked back up the dock into the Breezeby. I watched through the plate glass. She went right up to the hostess who was still staring at us as if we were a movie playing on the windshield of the boiling truck and said something to her and the woman said something obviously smart-assed back which was a mistake because my sister pointed her cigarette at the hostess's face and then the hostess went off and my sister stood there smoking until the woman came back and handed her something in looked like an envelope and then my sister Angie walked out of the Breezeby past the retard candy and the free real estate magazines and blew out of the door and into the parking lot. Never once did she look back at us watching from the dock. This was the last time I ever laid eyes on my foul-mouthed sister.

EIGHT

THE NOISE OF HOME crackled in my head like the static of an album where the needle catches in the last groove. The arm tries to lift itself off the album but when it sticks like that you have to put everything aside, nudge it slightly—not too hard or it will ruin the song—with your finger. You got to bygod act upon it.

Me and Tank, men of action, marching inland in the boiling sun, against the tide of pickups pulling boats, campers, vans with beach chairs, and coolers bungeed up on luggage racks. It must have been Friday, judging by the beach traffic. I'm no good at calendars. I only knew it was hot and I was tired and Tank was heavy as halfway across the drawbridge I had to piggyback him when he up and stopped walking. The sun boiling, beachgoers streaming by, Tank clutching his bag of army men. He'd got mad at me earlier for running Angie off which he said was my fault and then she beat it out of the parking lot into the sandy lot and over the PROTECTED NO TRESPASSING sand dunes without a look back or a last fuck y'all.

"I am going to beat your ass," he said, after I got him to stop screaming her name.

"You and whose army?" I said.

What shut him up was he never heard the expression and had to right then and there have it explained to him. Obviously he'd not reached that point in his schooling where all you learn is *your mama* trash talk. My daddy was no good at math but the local schools did allow him to commit to memory twenty uninterrupted minutes of the infamous legend of Dolomite of which we could only hear three or four sanitized verses. He claimed black guys taught it to him during shop class when they were supposed to be building bleachers for the new stadium. The woman he married, may she rest in peace, maintained he made it up himself. For some reason she could not fathom such a story passed down orally over generations in parking lots and mechanic's bays and lunchrooms by kids who could scarcely read. Then again, aside from Aretha, she could take or leave music which we all know what that means.

"Me and this right here army," said Tank after I explained the phrase, shaking his bag of green men.

Crossing the drawbridge, trying to drown out that stuck record static, I thought of learning Dolomite from my daddy next time he's All Clear and teaching it in turn to Tank. Then I made a list of all the other things I'd like to teach him in the short time we had left. I knew it would not be but days before they came and took Tank away if we showed up home. I knew I had to go look for Carter though, now that Angie and the woman my daddy married were lost to us.

THINGS I NEED TO TEACH TANK:
— Difference between Stax/Volt and Motown
— A little bit of Dolomite: the legend of
— Some manners?
— East north south west
— How to light the pilot on the furnace which it's always me lights it every fall
— Pee and brush your teeth at same time so you don't miss bus
— Beef stew recipe I got off the back of a can of tomato soup
— He knows it already but the coral snake rhyme

I thought of stories to tell Tank my daddy and some even my mother had told me, I thought of songs he needed to know, though he already knew more about music at his age than most people four times it. I wanted him to know that even though I would not actually physically right-beside-him be there always, I wasn't about to ever let him totally alone. I'd feel it if he was hungry or hurting, I'd know if he needed me, and wherever it was I happened to be I'd—no, I won't going to tell him this, I wasn't going to go promising something I could not deliver, I've always hated worse than her leaving the way my mama used to tuck us in nights with her big promises.

Al Green came on the waves, "Let's Stay Together." I started singing it aloud, Tank bobbing heavy on my shoulders, thinking I'd teach Tank that you could be walking down a Bulkhead backstreet and get whisked into a store looks like auto parts on the outside and up in the dim windowless inside, heavenly voices sing sweetly of the light in this world. When you are in need, the lights in this world line up to dice through the darkness, illuminate your path: magic caster, kindly Mexican, church lady, Streetclothes, moneylending trucker, what links them? Just knowing a traveler's in need, Tank.

I said I was talking about forever.

"And ever," said Tank.

"A pot of boiling grits!" I said as we came to the end of "Let's Stay Together."

"In his dang lap, what I mean," said Tank.

All our singers of songs suffered. You can hear the light in their voices, though, the sweetness of having survived. Nothing like song to breathe air into a puncture.

It wasn't so hard as I thought to get a ride with two because one was a pipsqueaky boy in camping britches swinging a bag of plastic army men. Sing your aria, Tank! Backed by a cast of thousands, yes sir, who cares if they're armed and green. A couple picked us up. We hummed up their Taurus and it shamed me to have to do so. So me and Tank told them a joke.

"Two peanuts were walking down the road," I said.

"One was a salted," Tank chimed in, perfectly timed, high-pitched, earnest.

"What do Eric Clapton and McDonald's . . ." he started after they laughed politely but I shushed him and kicked his knee. These old people didn't know no Eric Clapton. They were middle-aged country. Churchers, I'd say, out doing the Lord's work picking up two stray boys though they never in our face testified. I say bless them for stopping as many a God-fearing man and woman had switched lanes when they seen us obviously dirty and wild-haired boys standing on the shoulder just out of Bottomsail. Carter's hair was his favorite thing about himself. He told us many times. My sister Angie had turned beautiful but it was meanness which burned off her baby fat. The couple drove us all the way to Moody Loop. I called on Reverend Al Green for another lift up your hearts in song. Here is where things tend to jumble and collide. You will pardon me if it comes back to me aswirl. Al Green found Jesus after the pot of boiling grits. The girl who dropped them in his lap went in the other room and shot herself. I never told Tank this part of the story, just the pot-of-boiling-grits-in-the-lap part. She had a history of mental problems said my daddy with the straightest face. As if he was telling us she hailed from Terre Haute, Indiana. I did not tell Tank everything. For instance, what kind of sickness it was in my daddy's head and why our mother left us. For a minute we stood at the intersection of 692 and Moody Loop as if waiting for the school bus while I wondered whether to tell him about the house fire. Burned to the ground. Charred bricks and ash. He didn't need to be worrying about her coming back for him. It was the right thing to do. Angie knew.

"I'm hungry, can we go to Frosty's?"

"We're almost home," I said.

"I want Frosty's."

"We can't go to Frosty's."

"How come?"

"He don't like us anymore."

"Why not?"

"Just forget it Tank, okay?"

"But I want Frosty's."

I was fixing to slap him. I called on the Reverend Al Green. He winged in sweetly, "Call Me" interrupting all the buzz in my head. I sang it loud I sang it proud. It gave me the courage to put one foot in front of the other. Tank followed me on down Moody Loop. I had no idea what we'd find. Carter's hair carpeting the porch boards, the lobe of his left ear lost among the curls he so treasured. Banana stems and peelings, the fluffing from the mattress, Daddy is snowing and so am I.

So too were the fields, white with cotton. What a beautiful day it was, the sky so crisp, the fields curved slightly, the way farmland looks in children's books. I'm so tired of being alone. Call me, come back home. Tank had this book I used to read to him in which you left the bustle of the city on one page and on the next traveled country mouse out to the boonies which were so clean and spacious, miles of fields gently rolling and curved neatly as tucked bedsheets into low stone walls and bordering brooks. Silos and bright red barns, green tractors, farmers dressed in overalls and flannel shirts.

Where were the lagoons of hog waste that gagged us when the wind blew? The ravines with all grades of shit dumped down them, from pickles to sectional sofas? Goitered old women cussing at chickens in grassless yards, trailers listing on cinder blocks which one day while we were at school blew into a thousand pieces, some parolee's batch of crystal gone wrong.

Oh what a glorious day. Dusty mutts bounded down the farmhouse lanes to herald our triumphant return. Red flags on mailboxes saluted us.

Oh Angie fuck you too, girl, I love you, you foul-mouthed bitch.

I breathed to four-barreled life a half-one-thing/half-the-other which hybrids, now that I was far enough away to think about it, made some serious sense, seeing as how it's never wholly car nor truck. I believed I almost had an answer to Tank's question had stumped me for all those years. It seemed like the answer was waiting in the woods just off Moody Loop.

On the dashboard of my daddy's truck: receipts, wobbly old water-stained cigarette, coffee stirrer from sucks-without-Eric-Clapton McDonald's, withdrew-against-doctor's-advice papers, prescriptions for pills he don't take because he says he ain't living his life that way, feeling like a big chunk of potato in a thickly whisked batch of potato onion soup.

"I'm hungry," said Tank. I smiled at his timing, potato onion soup up in my head.

"We're almost there."

"I got to go too."

"Can you hold it?"

Of course he could not. We left the road, veered into the cornfield. Tank wanted to go between the rows but I made him keep walking. It's a matter of pride. We followed a drainage ditch to a stand of trees. Number two, said Tank. First, I said, I'm no good at math. But he looked so lost and pained so I told him since we're almost home just take your underpants off, use them to wipe with. I walked up into the rows, left him squatting and grimacing, ashamed for him and angry that I had to think about what number it was and what he ought to use to clean himself. I don't like to think or talk about such. Nobody ever talked to me about it. Listen to this, Joel Junior, my daddy would say when I was littler than Tank and for some reason inconsolable; he would drop the needle down on old Eddie Holman, "Hey There Lonely Girl," and according to legend I would settle all soothed down in seconds. I stood looking up the road. A Dr Pepper truck blew past. Dust trailed it like the noxious fumes of the mosquito man. Tank when I looked back to check on him was assiduously cleaning himself with his worn-only-once Fruit of the Looms. His intensity scared and depressed me. But it was an oh lovely day, straight out of a children's book. In a field off Moody Loop. Tank calling me asking me some question I couldn't hear. Inside or outside? A song rose out of the woods. Not the Reverend Al Green nor "Hey There Lonely Girl" which memory had brought back a snippet of, then drowned out as if I'd lost the signal between the rows of corn. Not the diminishing rumble of the Dr Pepper truck. This song rose out of the same woods bordering the back of our house. Tank was hollering at me. Finally I heard him. I don't like to think or talk about such. Nobody ever talked to me about it. "What do I do with them?" he hollered again.

Then the song washed over him so I could not answer. When I turned to look back at the woods the song died out. Like one of those movies where the babysitter hears something in her closet but when she opens the door it's just dresses boxes and shoes. I turned to look up the road and here came the song, low in the background, familiar as that same-ass cactus.

Y'all go outside and play, my mama said. How to stop your mind from going where it believes it ought to be? You summon up the words of Streetclothes: the one thing we can't do is make somebody feel the way they ought to feel.

Tank came up alongside me slapping himself on the neck. I stood there and watched him with all the sound turned down except that song, seeping out of the woods. What was it called? I tried to picture the album cover. Tank's mouth was moving.

"What is it?"

"A fuck mosquito," he said, slapping. He didn't know how to cuss yet, despite having spent some quality time with his sister.

"It's fucking," I corrected. "A fucking mosquito. Do you hear that music?"

"What music?"

"Nothing."

"No, what music?"

I said nothing.

"What music?"

"Goddamn it, Tank," I said. I hauled off and slapped him. Mosquitoes rose off him in a cloud. I slapped until his skin was pink. He stood there wailing but he didn't run. Who was he going to run to? Carter climbed down out of that truck and look what happened to Carter. I was awful to Carter sometimes but not really to Carter, he was just standing in, he didn't know that though. I told him if he didn't hold the pee bottle he could go back inside, hang with daddy. He turned his head and held the god-durn bottle.

Then the most beautiful music rose from the woods. The sun came out from behind a cloud and Jesus could not have come up with a finer light in this world. Tree leaves strained it. Dust danced in its shafts.

The song was about the drift atop daddy's dashboard. It was about the no *d* Promise Land. You blew in a tube under a dashboard and the song roared to life. Then you climbed in it and floored it, pedal to the metal, and it took you where ever you wanted to go.

Climb in, Tank. I'm tired of being alone.

Down past the silos and bright red barns, the green tractors, muddy Moody Loop transformed. We were almost home. Tank talking to me but I could not hear him for the song I inhabited as much as it inhabited me. I knew it but could not call its name. Guitar baptized in a back-roads church, praise the Lord chords soaked in rotgut from some downtown juke, a song that would leave grease stains on the walls of any room where you played it. Organ chords swirling in like waves down at Bottomsail. A woman lifting her voice high up to Heaven, singing about parts of her way south of the border and what done happened when she left somebody and how she had wandered the ends of the earth feeling low and could not find nothing to fill the hole in her heart and here she was fixing to come back home. Glorious homecoming sound track. Do you hear it, Tank?

But Tank didn't hear jack. I had slapped the ever-loving hell out of that boy. Mosquitoes had swarmed him and his skin was red from my slapping and puffing up welts from the bites. He was sweaty and crying, his whole head soaked. We stood in the middle of Moody Loop. There is where I woke up, a breeze winging in the odor of hog lagoon.

I had to carry Tank the last half mile. He wasn't talking to me. How could I explain the music in my head, that wood song seeping? I tried to get him back with the O'Jays "Love Train." A train had come for us earlier and I'd promised not to get on it but looked like I had and took him with me. Then I learned how not to love. I left him with my sister and went to Bulkhead. I went off by myself and it was for myself. I got good at love. But there was nothing in it but loneliness and Tupperwared leftovers.

I tried to get Tank to catch that train.

From above a weak little whiny monotone declaring tell them all in Israel too.

We ran alongside the tracks and caught finally the chorus, climbed up on that love train, love train.

I looked for smoke above the trees. Maybe they'd died in a fire also. Then I remembered I hadn't told Tank. I couldn't remember why not. I couldn't remember what was a lie and what actually had happened. I just could not remember. We'd been gone only two days and it seemed like months. We wore the same pants but were changed. We hummed and were hungry and we shat in the cornfield and threw brand-new underwear in the drainage ditch. There were no green silos, only the swamp sulking on one side of the house, those smoky woods on the other from which that song once again seeped, so low I could barely hear it.

That reminded me. I told Tank some Tank jokes.

"Would you like me to sing a solo?"

"So low I can't hear you, that's fine with me," said Tank.

"How about, would you like me to sing tenor?"

"Ten or fifteen miles away please," said Tank.

I could not see Tank's face but I could hear him smiling above me. We passed alongside those woods, the song growing louder. She'd left and been gone, now here she was coming on back down home. Then it seemed like the song got stuck. We passed alongside the cactus woods and then the fields and then those same-ass cactus woods. Save me save me save me, sang my songstress. We were almost there and almost there.

"What's wrong, Joel Junior? Why we stopping?"

You could stop and keep going. Wasn't it weird, the way you could stop walking and keep walking in your head?

He was on my shoulders still. He was the jockey and I was the horse on the home stretch. Wasn't anybody betting on my tired ass, you got that right.

There it was, our daddy's house. No smoke, no charred brick and ash. No POLICE LINE DO NOT CROSS. Frosty never did call any law. People are too stuck up behind their counters to be anybody else's savior. It's like I told Sheriff Deputy Rex, you got to go ahead, do it yourself, don't lie in bed awake forever worrying why did you not. No pickup parked out in the no-tree-plantedest yard in the whole state. A common criminal was likely driving it up and down the beach in Bulkhead, Tank's remnant Ruffle dust lingering in the cab, my daddy's *Top of the Stax* tape on the box.

I felt Tank tense above me. I tried to pick him off my shoulders but his knees clamped around my neck. We had two dismounts established from prior shoulderings: regular, in which I simply lifted him off and set him down, and fancy, a flip-off with a circus ring flourish.

"Fancy or regular?" I asked.

"No," he said like a three-year-old. Mostly *n*s in it, hardly any *o*.

"You got to get off," I said.

We stood in the yard, his knees clamped around my neck. That song building up now. Coming on home to you, she sang. I tried to argue with her. Home to whom? I said. But I

couldn't be arguing with her. She was the light in this world.
She was the green silos the shafts of dusty light the whistle
you blow to crank the hybrid. She was another in a long line
of saviors: Frosty bless his fat, bag-flapping self, kindly Mexican, magic caster, I don't need to go through the whole list
again, y'all got it, she was the last, she'd delivered me and
Tank too, though he claimed he couldn't hear her. I did not
know then how good it was that he heard only his own quick-
ened breath and maybe the breeze through the trees of those
surly woods.

"Is anybody home?" He whispered this. It felt like something he wanted to holler though, some line he'd heard on
TV before my daddy golfclubbed it.

I edged up in the yard. Close enough to see the golden
locks of Carter's hair carpeting the porch boards. I thought,
If I can just find that earlobe. Then I thought, And do what
with it? I had heard you could attach a severed something-
another if you scooped it up and took it along with you to the
emergency room but I imagined it was a time limit on it and,
besides, I wasn't the one going to save anybody, I'd run off
and left that boy to the care of my daddy with a pair of scissors in his hand.

"You stay out here in the yard," I told Tank.

"No," he said, clamping tighter.

"Join hands then," I sang.

We were so tall. What would my daddy look at us and see?
A eight-foot two-headed cyborg alien robot? I didn't like it

one bit. But I could not get Tank down off of me. I had took him to raise. His little legs liked to strangled me. We picked our way across the porch boards, through my brother Carter's hair, which muffled our footfalls. The woodsong of my savior drowning out the O'Jays, I tried to search for that lobe but you could say I was distracted.

Tank smelled gamey like little boys do when they play outside and don't never wash. He hummed and his legs were clammy. He went to wildly scratching his legs. "Stop it," I whispered to him, and Lord God Almighty he actually stopped.

The door was open. We stood at the screen. It was rusty and inside was dark and all I could see at first was the row of albums stretched across the wall. I had missed our music. But I didn't need it because I had it all in my head. I was thankful for that gift. I was for a few seconds full of praise for that song inside my head.

But then it got louder. So I pulled open the screen door. The inside of the house smelled at first like ashes left in the hearth heated up by the first hot spring day, then more like the inside of someone's mouth. It was dark and the windows were closed and then it hit you how it wasn't bad breath but something else far deeper down and more awful. I tried to take Tank down and he would not come off of me. I said, Get down now, Tank, and he said, No, and I tried to pry his legs off me and he wouldn't let go. His legs were pinching my neck so hard I couldn't breathe good. I was gasping and trying to pull his legs off and that little fucker had some kind of superhero cartoon strength shooting through him. I could not get him off of me. He liked to choked me to death. We were struggling and making all sorts of racket. This won't good, this was real real bad. We needed to get back aboard that train. One train left because I let it and then we left and another brought us back but then we got off and as soon as we did I wanted back on.

Carter came out on the porch and called to us. He ain't even in here, he said. Me and Tank sat in the shut tight pickup and I felt like a fool for staying out there all day long in the boiling sun with nothing to eat but Pop Rocks and Nabs when he ain't even in there. But Carter didn't come out from his room where he was maybe reading comic books or playing with army men up under his bed. He must be gone too, else he'd of heard our mess and come running.

Sheriff Deputy Rex come and got him, I thought, and it's a good thing he did. I wondered why I didn't let him take us months ago when she left us here with him but then I remembered how it was when my daddy was All Clear. I remembered how good people can be. Light in this world. Baby it's good to see you, sang my songstress. Lord I'm glad to be back home, she sang, and then here come the organ, unrolling its thick chords like carpet across the floor of the front room, knocking over all the records, slapping the warped floorboards of the farmhouse, get out the way now, here it comes, that song again which then I recognized it for what it was: that song out of my daddy's head.

He must of come in while we were struggling. I didn't

even hear him for the song. If Tank heard him he didn't let on until he spoke to us, "Hey there, Joel Junior, hey, Tank," and we turned and there he stood behind us, the screen door slapping against his backside, a smile on his face.

"Where y'all been?"

Tank was shaking. He still had those knees so tight I could hardly breathe, much less talk. I wasn't so much in the mood to talk to him anyhow. I wondered what we ever come back there for.

"We were just down to Frosty's for some snacks," I whispered from between Tank's knees.

He was wearing work pants and a white T-shirt. Same thing I'd seen him in last. The T-shirt was splotched with blood. His face was so dirty there were streaks of clean from where sweat had run down him. Otherwise his face was nearly black in places, from where it looked like he'd rubbed it in the mud.

He was staring at my chest. He looked up at me and smiled.

"Mario, hey? I like that. Y'all seen my truck?"

Tank, I could tell, was warming to him. He had loosened his legs around my neck. But it was that same-ass cactus. He might be All Clear now but that cactus was going to crop back up directly. If this is love I'm joining the motherfucking carnival.

"Y'all go outside and play," I said to Tank.

"Who's y'all?" my daddy said. "And where's my truck, Joel Junior?"

I hated he called me that. I hated him and loved him too. It won't his fault, and it won't mine. People do they best they can except when they don't and then they claim to have been doing the best they can. Tank let me dismount him regular, not fancy. Fancy given the circumstances would have seemed a little frivolous I believe.

"Go outside for a minute," I told Tank.

"I want you to come with me."

"I'll take you out there," I said. "Then I'm coming back in."

My daddy smiled at us through his streaky face. Dried mud lining his forehead cracked when he smiled.

I took Tank by the hand and led him out to the yard. We kept going past where the truck was before I stole it. I led him out to the road. I told him stand right there in the middle of Moody Loop and wait for me. He said something but I couldn't hear him over that song. I kneeled down and hugged him. Holy Moly that boy hummed.

"I love you, Tank, you know I love you," I said.

"I love you, Mario," said Tank.

"Look," I said. "If I don't come out and daddy does, you just race him, okay? I bet you can beat him in a race."

"How far a race?"

"Up to the Jackson's trailer house."

"That's too far."

"He can take you in a short race but not all the way up to the Jackson's."

"I can beat him," Tank said.

"Just go right inside, tell Mrs. Jackson I said let you stay with her for a while, okay? Wait there for me and if I don't come ask her to call Sheriff Deputy Rex."

"Ain't it a race anymore?"

"No," I said. "Not when you get there. Then it's just an errand."

"I guess so," said Tank. He seemed disappointed that a race would end up an errand. I hated to disappoint that boy. He always had good questions but when he went to asking them more often than not I'd just get ill at him. I'd slap the bejesus out of him. Bejesus, if he's the same as Jesus, he can't be all bad as there's a sweetness in the songs that bear his name. Maybe he's just in those songs and that's all and that's enough.

What it was, when I walked back up in the yard, all the songs I loved seemed like they were playing at once. I could not hear jack. Like someone was twisting the tuning dial on the radio. I'd hear a note or two from Sly, then same from the Staples, Reverend Al, Marvin, J. B., Aretha. I even heard some white boys my daddy thought could sing some soul music: Steve Marriott, Van Morrison, Eric Burdon. I heard it all, organ, bass, chicken-peck gospel guitar, I heard drums and sax and trumpet, Otis called to me from the deep of a Wisconsin lake, Al Green hollered when those boiling grits hit his lap. I felt for all my sweet singers who came to sad ends, but Marvin Gaye, his was the death that got away with me the most. I could not hardly listen to him knowing he was shot by his own flesh and blood while he'd gone off.

My daddy was sitting in his chair. He had put on an album. He was playing Sam and Dave. Sam and Dave were singing "Let It Be Me." I stood there a minute, trying to tell Sam from Dave, but I could not.

"Where's Carter?" I said.

"Carter?" My daddy had his eyes half-closed. Looked like he was drifting off to sleep sitting up.

"Yeah, Carter. You know, Carter?"

My daddy's eyes struggled to stay open. He sang along with Sam or Dave, whichever one it was, didn't matter, it was the same song.

"Carter needed a haircut. I gave him a haircut, then he went to sleep out in the hammock."

I did not want to leave that room. It smelled bad the farther you went back in the house. I did not want to go to the kitchen where the bad smell was coming from. I was thinking I'd stay in that room and listen to the song out of my daddy's head which wasn't "Let It Be Me," it was that wood song. But then I remembered Tank outside and I turned around and watched him through the screen door draw something in the dirt of Moody Loop with a stick he'd found. I looked over at my daddy and all I heard was Sam and Dave. I thought about my mama saying it wasn't nothing that would dare inhabit a child and I decided I'd bygod believe her and believe that she was just doing the best she could and that if she wasn't doing too good it was because she wasn't capable of any more.

I left my daddy nodding out there in the chair. Down the dark hallway it smelled worse the farther you got. And in the kitchen good God Almighty. Blood had dripped all over the

floor there and led in a dried trickle to the back door. I felt
Tank's legs around my neck, choking me. For some reason I
thought of Carla and her slutty self. Me and her were slow-
dancing to Otis, "Pain in My Heart." I did not look down anymore. The light in this world buzzed outside the kitchen,
through the rusty screen. I pushed open the screen and saw
Carter in the hammock but smelled him before I ever got
outside good. I pulled blessed Mario up over my mouth and
stood there on the back porch. Carter was sagging in that
hammock, so heavily the ropes nearly touched the pine
straw. The three of us used to get up in that hammock and it
never drooped that low. I saw all his hair had been clipped
off. I saw from the porch the cuts on his head and the flies
and bugs feeding on him. It was an oh lovely day. Babies
claim their name is Mario when really it is Joel Junior. I
heard nothing at all but the wind in the pine needles.

I put my hand in my back pocket and felt something in
there. I pulled out me and Tank's temporary tattoos we'd
bought at the surf shop with my sister's leftover money.
Wasn't that a year ago that we'd wandered around that surf
shop laying hands on smooth boards and I had out of pride
bought something from surly Glenn? It seemed like I had
covered so many thousand miles. Strength and Good Judgment, read my temporary tattoo. Peace and Tranquility, said
Tank's. It made my stomach roll how I had not the strength
and good judgment to affix Tank's tattoo to his little pipsqueaky bicep so that peace and tranquility might follow him
this day and all his livelong ones forever and ever let us praise

bejesus. I carried the words around just like I did the key to the pickup in my pocket. It made me actually sick to remember how I sat in that boiling pickup all day long, the keys in my pocket, talking to my high-up-in-some-hotel mama about basement or attic instead of driving my brothers to someplace safe. Everything I needed to save us all stuck up in my pocket.

I pulled Mario back down off so I could hurl. It wasn't anything on my stomach but thick yellow water. I don't like to think or talk about such. It was a horrible noise arising out of my belly. I tried to summon some other song but it was only that ugliest retching aria in the air around me. It's a wonder I even still know the names of all the sweet songs I grew up on but do you know to this day even after all that happened down off Moody Loop I play the records my daddy bought at Dusselbach's, I sing in my head those songs he loved and that I love too. Somebody might say, I don't know how you can stand to listen to that mess but they just don't know how glad I was to learn I did not share the song in his head. I could hear it but I did not understand note one of it.

Then this happened: Tank got tired of waiting. He came up on the front porch and peeked through the screen and seen in the chair our daddy half sort of sleeping. Thank Jesus he had enough sense to leave him be. He came around the house on the swamp side keeping close upside it. Red-yellow-black, stay way back. When he saw Carter, Tank went to wailing. Nothing like I ever heard out of him before. I wasn't through heaving up nothing—the lining of my belly's what it felt like — but I had to stop my own mess and go be some-body's big brother.

Pardon me now if it comes back to me aswirl. Tank went to wailing but not wailing, it was like nothing I'd ever heard out of his mouth. I had an older sister she left she couldn't take it. Dizzy and sick I grabbed Tank and tried to shush him. There is no *d* in Promise Land because it's only love that can kill you down there, not house fires. Houses live both inside and outside at once and I have Tank to thank for asking the question in the first place and sorry-ass Landers for leading me to the answer by way of a half-car/half-ugly-truck. That was the trick, to keep it warm or cool inside like my dream basement but weather also the outward storms. I wanted to tell Tank but Tank was screaming and squirming and I clamped my hand over his mouth and wrestled him around the corner of the house. I have been old and I'm no younger now for having told this story but I'll say one thing and that is: she gave up, but he was just following orders. I was weak from no sleep and a diet of garbage food but Tank had the supercurrent surging through him. All day long I sat in the boiling trunk with those truck keys lumped in my pocket like a hard-on I stroked and teased and saved as if some sweet girl was going to get a lift out to Moody Loop in the late afternoon. Tank knows I could have driven us all to someplace safe. He knows the windshield was a movie screen and that I'd just soon sing some Curtis as keep Carter from climbing out of that truck. Tank knows I kept Carter up on that porch with a scissors-wielding daddy. He sure does know

I left his ass down at Bottomsail in the care of our sister who left, she couldn't take it, if this is love. Oh it was going on the loveliest day I'd ever in my whole life seen. I wrestled Tank up in my arms and he squirmed down out of my hold. I caught up to him around the swamp side of the house. We were moving along, Tank flailing, when our daddy came around the side of the porch. We could either go back to where Carter lay dead and humming in the slung-low hammock or shoot off into the swamp. I put Tank down or tried to. After all that wriggling and screaming he was clamped to me again. But it would not do, the both of us running from him.

"Tank, get down now, let me talk to him."

"No," said Tank. "What did he do to Carter, what's wrong with Cart?"

"It's no time to talk," I whispered to him. I had been so old. Won't no point in whispering, my daddy was standing waiting for us at the edge of the porch. He could have heard us but from the look of him, mud-streaked face, cloudy eyes, he'd gone off again or more than likely never had come back on. Had he, he'd of turned himself in when he found Carter in the hammock and us missing. He'd have wondered if he did the same to us as Carter. He don't remember a thing afterward. He would have called Sheriff Deputy Rex and said come get me. He was a good man my daddy. At least he has an excuse. You'd think I'd of learned to forgive him but nothing fucks you up like loving another person. They list all those means of death, call it cancer or AIDS, high blood pressure or blunt trauma, but it's one and only love that lays

you out in a dark daytime grave. Tank let me put him down
but clung to my legs.

"Go around through the kitchen," I told him. "Bring me
a butcher knife."

"No," said Tank. He went to hiccuping then. It about
made me laugh as it always did, his little chest leaping from
the bubbling inside. But I did not laugh as I wished for Tank
a lifetime of Peace and Tranquility. Daddy just stood there
mud-streaky smiling. We could have run into the swamp but
it was lousy with snakes to where we had to screen the chim-
ney or they'd climb down into the fireplace and you'd find
them coiled in the dark cool corners. I miss old Moody Loop
sometimes. Even it if smelled like hog lagoon, even it was
lousy with snakes and mosquitoes and black sucking sand.
The songs in my head spill right out of that house back down
on Moody Loop where my daddy stood lost listening to the
voices which came on over whatever else he'd been listening
to. If he was fixing to do to one of us what he did to Carter,
let it be me. "Go on, Tank, now," I said, and I pushed him
and he took off running up the side of the house. I believe
the sudden movement is what jarred my daddy. Maybe he
was so gone off he could only distinguish vague shapes and
movement. He started down toward me. I thought to lead
him in the swamp where surely the coral snakes would set
upon him and him too off to remember the rhyme would
confuse them with the common harmless corn snake just
like when I returned to Moody Loop from my worthless jour-
ney and could not distinguish between my daddy back from

one of his voyages and him still way the hell off. Everybody knows it I was born this way. In the fourteen years I spent down off Moody Loop I'd never laid eyes on a single coral snake. "Red-yellow-whatever, who gives a fuck, I've never seen one and neither has any of y'all," said my foul-mouthed sister. She was right, it was a song we sang, an evil we nearly coveted, but it never came and we spent our youths cowering from it. I just stood there. Let it be me. Tired of waiting, bring it on. I could feel my little brother's appendages still clinging to me, phantom limb pain I believe is how they refer to that phenomenon. Though it was technically not *my* limbs lopped off, that boy was a part of me. Severed pink lobe falling through the dusty shafts of oh so lovely light. I offered no resistance when my daddy tackled me and put his hands around my throat. I figured it was what I deserved for keys up in my all-day-long pocket, for turning out so bad at love. He ground my face in the mud so that I looked just like him. She named me after him after all. For so long I worried that my daddy and I shared that same song, the one playing in his head which I was close enough to hear buzzing. I thought I would miss Tank and Carter and especially those songs playing in my head which would soon enough stop. The thought that the music would stop is what must of made me momentarily fight back enough to turn my head upward toward the lovely sky and see Tank come up behind my daddy from the front porch side and stick the knife in his back. My daddy turned around clawing at Tank which left me free to scramble up and kick him hard in the head but

Tank had somehow hit just right, low and to the side so that it missed bone but struck organ.

Me and Tank watched our daddy fall half-in/half-out of the swamp. We stood there watching him spasm and heave. Then he made a sound like train's brakes sighing. I stepped over him and reached for Tank. We joined hands. We ran alongside the tracks and caught finally the chorus: all aboard the love train, love train.